Marital Rites

MARGARET FORSTER

Marital Rites

Secker & Warburg · London

First published in England 1981 by
Martin Secker & Warburg Limited,
54 Poland Street, London WIV 3DF

British Library Cataloguing in Publication Data

Forster, Margaret
    Marital rites.
    I. Title
    823'.914[F]   PR6056.0/

    ISBN 0–436–16112–5

Printed and bound in Great Britain by
Morrison & Gibb Ltd, London and Edinburgh

For Marion and Jeffrey Pitt

One

Anna Osgood remembered what she had said very well. Nobody would need to remind her, should they be so cruel. The sound of her own voice returned to her, abnormally strident, much too shrill, she knew, shouting defiance in that small, cluttered kitchen where they had been sitting. She remembered taking a huge gulp of coffee before she began, knowing she had a lot to say. And she had said it, all of it.

"It makes me sick, *sick*," she had begun, "every time I think of it. How you can all sit there and go on about how absolutely marvellous she's been – praising her, actually praising her! I don't admire her in the least. She's stupid, just accepting it like that, just condoning what he has done, not making the least attempt to do anything about it. Oh shut up, do, I know exactly what you're about to say, Gillian – you're going to say she had no alternative. Well, I don't agree with that either. There are always alternatives. She just sat down and snivelled and then gave up. And now she goes around with that dreadful suffering look," (Gillian had managed to interrupt that time with, "But Anna, she *is* suffering,") "and not doing anything to stop it. If you fall down and cut yourself you don't just lie there, do you? You don't let sleeping dogs lie, do you?" ("You do if you're half dead, Anna.") "And – and – oh, you know what I mean, I've got lost in my own metaphors as usual. But I can't take it, I just can't. I *despise* her."

A chorus in praise of Elizabeth had followed. The others – Gillian and Lucy – they had both wallowed in a sentimental fashion in Elizabeth's bravery. Elizabeth had shielded the children, they said. She had gone on working. She had acted as though nothing had happened. "Oh!" Anna had shouted, enraged, "but something *had* happened. My God – her marriage had been shattered – twenty-two years crushed to pieces and she just accepted it. She should have screamed and roared and given him hell." And how angry she had been when Gillian had said, "But she was civilised, she behaved in a civilised fashion."

"Then she shouldn't have," Anna had gone on, working herself into a frightful state. "People should not be civilised, I don't admire it at all. I'm sick of all this polite behaviour, letting him come and collect his things, keeping out of the way when he did it, sending his mail on, letting the children visit him and his disgusting little tart, actually defending him to them – it's ridiculous. And now she's just letting him have a divorce, just like that, not making any trouble, doing everything she can to help and inside she's bottling up all this agony –"

They had both interrupted then, a chorus, a regular wail of "But what else could she have done?" She had told them what Elizabeth could have done. She closed her eyes and imagined her red angry face as she had told them. "What could she have done? She could have fought, like women should. She could have used every advantage she had. She could have gone straight round and hit him and brought him to his senses. No, I am *not* being silly. He needed a shock, he needed to see the horror of what he was doing. And then she should have refused to help at all, she should have blocked everything he wanted to do at every step. She should never have left his side, morning, noon or night. She should have gone to his office, followed him to lunch, just generally have made his life hell. What he's done is criminally insane and she should have treated him exactly like a criminal. She should have hounded him. What good would it have done? It would have made him realise that what he was doing was barbaric. How does he know now what this 'civilised' behaviour is costing her? He doesn't. He hasn't the imagination. He's probably even convinced himself she's actually quite glad. I've a good mind to go and see him myself."

Of course, she hadn't. They had all been appalled – interference of such a blatant kind was quite out of the question. They had remonstrated with her without using the tired words, "Mind your own business." And Gillian, always the more positive of the two, had said it was all very well for her to talk like that. "You're being smug, Anna," she had said. "Oh yes, you are. You know you're not likely ever to be in that position. Elizabeth's marriage was never like your own and you know that perfectly well. Peter had had affairs before. This had been coming for a long time and Elizabeth probably suspected it – well, I know she suspected it. She was facing up to the inevitable. It's no good pretending they were married for twenty glorious years like you and Robert. They weren't glorious. They may not even have been worth saving. Not all marriages are."

Gillian had been married twice, so there was a respectful pause. Her first marriage, to a policeman, had ended in apparent tragedy when he was killed in a bank robbery. One of the most electrifying moments in Anna's sheltered life had been when she heard Gillian say, some years ago, in another kitchen, that she had never been so relieved in her life. For two of the five years of that marriage she had been having an affair with another man and she could hardly bear the sight of her husband. Anna, at the time, had not believed married women had affairs.

They had left Lucy's kitchen still arguing, Anna vigorously upholding her point of view. She remembered reaching her own home, across the road, and being surprised to find her hands hot and sweaty and trembling slightly. She knew what Gillian and Lucy would be saying to each other as they stood at the door a little longer, revelling in her extraordinary, uncharacteristic outburst. They would be saying she was naïve, that she was so protected by the happy facts of her own life that she didn't understand other people's problems. Lucy, trim in her flowered dress, would tighten her already taut stomach muscles (four babies and not an ounce of extra fat) and say that she just wondered what Anna and Robert's marriage was really like anyway. They were a legend, but how could one really know? And Gillian, strong, sensible, broad-of-beam Gillian, who knew perfectly well about Lucy's brief affair last summer, who knew Lucy wanted reassurance that her own flawed marriage was just as good as Anna's, Gillian would be loyal. She would say it had to be accepted: Anna and Robert were simply happy in their wonderfully lucky marriage and that was that.

But Anna, all that day, had felt acutely uncomfortable. She could not understand her own rage against Elizabeth. She wished already that she had not spoken out so violently — it was so very unlike her — and yet her anger had sprung from within her spontaneously. She hated to hear of Elizabeth's humiliation. It offended her in a personal way she found inexplicable. All around her she seemed to see marriages

4

threatened, broken, violated, marriages that were not really marriages, marriages in which deceit was commonplace and nobody thought anything of it. And Anna liked marriage. She thought it a wonderful institution and did not like to see it denigrated. Being married was the most important thing in the world to her. Marriage was sacred. The world – her world, the world in which she lived – had gone mad if it no longer thought so.

Anna dressed with extreme care. She had never become slovenly but it was not the custom in the circles in which she moved – very confined circles – to dress smartly. It was rather mocked. If one of them – Gillian, Lucy, Elizabeth or Anna herself – put on lipstick in the morning, the others would raise their eyebrows (unplucked) and a little light-hearted explaining would have to be done. They all had their styles, they all recognised deviations from the norm in each other. Anna's norm was jeans and a shirt or pullover and one of those padded cotton jackets from Clothkits which she had made herself. The jeans were never scruffy. She had four pairs, always immaculately laundered, unlike her daughter Sarah's, and she saw to it that they were fashionably cut. Her shirts and pullovers were always pretty and soft. She considered she looked quite good for a woman of forty-two.

But now she discarded her jeans, her workaday uniform, and put on her best green dress. It distressed her to find the dress a little tight. Her stomach hurt when she had pulled up the zip and fastened the belt and it did not hang as well as it had once done. She turned sideways. Really, the bulge round her tummy *was* minimal. When she had put on her high-heeled, fragile new shoes, the extra height they gave her further minimised the slight lumpiness round her middle, a lumpiness she was never normally aware of. She felt very confident as she put in her ear-rings. It was not that she

5

flattered herself into believing she was as attractive at forty-two as she had been at twenty-two, but she felt all the same very far from downtrodden or past it. She had seen photographs of Gillian at twenty, and the contrast with Gillian now was pathetic, quite pathetic. Once, she had tentatively broached the subject of putting on weight to Gillian but the result was not what she had expected. Yes, her friend had agreed, she knew she had put on weight but she saw no point in making herself miserable taking it off. She didn't think she ate too much and she got lots of exercise so it must just be her metabolism and had to be accepted. Anna, appalled at such a lack of self-honesty (Gillian grossly overate and drove everywhere), was speechless. With Lucy and Elizabeth, she agreed Gillian looked a sight and how could she bear it?

Anna brushed her hair vigorously. For years she had worn it long and loose but soon after her fortieth birthday she had had it cut. It had not been an easy decision. Her hair was one of her best features, a lovely dark auburn shade, and it was thick and glossy. Robert loved it spread out on a pillow: he had once said he could never love a woman with short hair. But the simple truth was that Anna looked at Lucy and saw herself reflected. Nobody over forty could successfully wear their hair tied up with a ribbon, flowing freely from it down an aging back. So she had taken a deep breath and had it cut, drastically. The hairdresser had pointed out that there were alternatives – Anna could learn to coil and braid and pin up her hair. He demonstrated. Anna saw how good she could look. But she had no skill in her fingers and knew that, like Lucy, she would continue to resort most days to bands and clips and ribbons and so she went ahead and had it cut. She saw at once she had made a very grave mistake.

Irritated, Anna put the brush down. Her close-cropped cap of hair looked neat, clean. That was all that was important. She disliked women who made a fuss about their looks or their clothes – clothes did not matter. She knew, of course, that her attitude was defensive and that this was why she protested lack of interest in fashion. She was not well dressed, never had been, she did not have a sense of style. It maddened her when she had to buy an outfit for a special occasion and realised how inept she was at putting things together. But fortunately Robert thought she looked lovely, always, and although she knew this was because he never really looked at her critically it was nevertheless consoling. He, too, had his priorities right. Sarah was different. To Anna, her elder daughter was a rag-bag, but she had picked up from others that Sarah was considered by her own weird generation to have style. And Sarah despaired of her mother's clothes. Anna read it in her eyes. Coming down the stairs, about to go out with Robert, she would say, "Well, we're off. How do I look?" "Fine," Sarah would say, "great," and instantly Anna would feel acutely miserable.

Well, she was ready. There was nothing else she could do to herself, nothing else worth doing, and anyway her appearance was not going to make the slightest scrap of difference in the ordeal ahead. She got into the car with a cheerful wave to Lucy, just turning the corner and off to Sainsbury's. She felt quite composed, in no danger of losing her considerable nerve. Worse things had happened. This was absolutely nothing compared to Imogen's accident. She sat very straight, a smile on her face, and concentrated hard on the traffic. It was only two years since she had passed her driving test. Robert had arranged lessons for her fortieth birthday as part of her approaching liberation from the ties of small children but though passing the test after only twelve lessons had been an unexpected triumph she had never really relaxed in the driver's seat. Robert drove with panache and she knew she never would.

Robert's publishing firm had recently moved from Soho to Wandsworth, a fact he never stopped cursing. He had liked working in Soho, liked walking round that area in his lunch hour when he first started, liked taking authors out to so many different restaurants later on. The move to Wandsworth had made him quite ill but the chairman had said facts must be faced. The lease was up, they could not afford to renew it at 1980 prices, so they would have to move out. The chairman, who lived in Putney, thought Wandsworth ideal. Robert, who lived in Highgate, thought it hell.

Crossing the river unnerved her, as it always did, but once she had turned into Westbridge Road she breathed easier. She was quite surprised to find she was not practising what she was going to say. It would all come out when she needed it. She had immense faith in her own articulacy. All that worried her was controlling it. Whatever happened, she must not – as she had done in Lucy's kitchen six months ago – she must not let anger fly out of herself without channelling it. The target was there. She must hit it, repeatedly.

Robert stood at the window of his office staring out at the rooftops. He missed the trees of Soho Square – it quite upset him, even now, to realise how much he missed them. George, the chairman of George Gusset and Crowther, said rooftops were more interesting and was amused at Robert's country yearnings. He knew Robert would in fact have liked to live in the country, that he spent every weekend at his cottage near Dedham, and he was always teasing Robert about being a village yokel at heart. Robert was perfectly happy to be teased. If Anna had agreed, if he was in almost any other profession but publishing, then he would indeed have lived in the country, far from any rooftops at all.

Robert felt ill and unhappy. Normally a vigorous, energetic man, he had been alarmed when he woke up in his awful hotel bedroom that morning to realise he was not himself. He tried to reassure himself that it was the hotel that was making him feel decidedly shaky and queasy – he loathed staying in hotels or indeed anywhere but his own bedroom. He was a bad guest in anybody else's house, and holidays were generally a misery at night. But it was more than the usual feeling of hotel-inspired irritation. His mouth was dry and his inside felt empty. He knew he was afraid.

It was a complicated emotion. This was not the fear of pain, nor the fear of retribution. What he was afraid of was himself. He was terrified that he had reached the stage of not knowing his own mind. He was afraid of total confusion. Always forthright and strong, he now felt utterly feeble, dizzy with the agony of not knowing what he should do. Or rather, what he should have done because now it was done.

It still seemed astonishing that it was. Not that the idea of confession was new: it had haunted him from the very first moment of his affair with Claire. He had quite literally woken up the next morning and found an apology framed in his mind – "Anna, darling, I've something terrible to tell you, I don't know how to begin, what to say, what happened was this." But he never got any further – "this" refused to clarify into any kind of adequate explanation. And then, when he returned home, the words seemed so phoney, they would not fit in anywhere, he could not slot them into the desultory chat of married life. He waited for Anna to help by saying, "You seem very quiet, what's the matter?" but she didn't say it, only said, "Tired?" and he said he was and could not add why. So it had gone on, the agonising words always in his head, the guilt in his heart, neither declared. It shook him to find infidelity so easy, outwardly. Why, there was nothing to it, so long as you had a loving and trusting wife to whom it was unthinkable to say what you wished to say. That was why, in the end, he had to resort to writing. Nobody needed to tell him how underhand a letter was, what an act of cowardice, what a relic of the Victorian era. But he himself felt like a relic of the Victorian era. Only on paper had he been able to formulate his thoughts and feelings. And of course he had never intended to send it. He had simply been sitting at his desk, towards the end of the afternoon, knowing he was going to meet Claire and then go home to Anna and suddenly it was too much. He found himself writing, "Dear Anna," and the rest flowed from him in a smooth and steady stream of words. He didn't stop for three pages and when at the end he read it through he was so relieved that at last his secret was out, that he had not only said what he wanted to say but also said it how he would have wished to say it. He couldn't have said it to Anna's face. Her eyes would have stopped him, he would have faltered, become confused. On paper, he was eloquent. Quickly, he had put his letter into the envelope and sealed it. Perhaps Anna too would benefit from facing the truth on paper. She would be able to digest the news better, be able to go back over what he had said when the first shock was over. At the thought of that shock he had winced, moved uneasily in his back-supporting swivel-chair. He could not be there when Anna got this letter. He would have to go away, not be in the house in the morning.

All night in his head he had read and re-read his own letter, anxiously examining it for faults. Perhaps he had said too much. He wished, on reflection, that he had not named Claire but the point of the letter was to be, at last, completely truthful and Claire was part of the complete truth. He wished also that he had not said so forcefully that he was afraid he did love her, that it was not just an affair. But then he had made it even more plain that he still adored Anna, that his love for her was in no way affected. He worried that he had tried to excuse himself too much, or that he had attempted to apportion blame when blame did not come into it. Perhaps by writing such a letter in office time he had sounded too businesslike and official but he knew that if he had tried to write it anywhere else he would have torn it up. He had given it to Betty to post to protect himself from doing just that, and then he had gone and spent an awful night in a cheap hotel, away from Anna, away from Claire, entirely alone. He had rung Anna, he had rung Claire, he had told them the same lie about having to go out of town.

His secretary, Betty, had told him to go home the minute he came in. "You look terrible, Robert," she said, (they were a modern office, no sirs or surnames). "Go straight home – I'll ring Anna and tell her you're on your way. I'm surprised she let you come, very surprised." Betty, a homely, dependable sort of girl to whom Robert was devoted even though she got on his nerves with her self-righteousness, was very surprised by most things. Her favourite compliment was to call people "mature", her favourite insult to call them "selfish". She was constantly very surprised at quite ordinary occurrences or patterns of behaviour and into her surprise was always written rebuke. Anna was rebuked for letting Robert come to work and Robert knew Betty longed to get on the telephone and push the rebuke home.

Betty proved hard to restrain, but he restrained her. He said he had a bug. Betty blushed furiously, a sign that she felt he was lying. She asked him if anything awful had happened. Imogen was well? (She had never forgiven him for not telling her Imogen had been in a car crash until the day after it happened.) He winced when she asked him, not wanting to think about Imogen for one solitary second – his sanity depended on not thinking about her – and she pounced on this visible sign of his distress to question him further.

Robert sat down again at his desk. Work was the best antidote to fear. No, it was knowledge that was the best antidote, but he had no knowledge, he felt utterly stupid, he had only work. Two manuscripts awaited his final decision. Out there in the wilderness two little novelists waited breathlessly for his yea or nay. He looked at the readers' reports, he looked at the agent's report, he looked at his own notes. Nothing seemed to matter any more. Fear so filled him that he was incapable of rational thought. Something would have to happen – it was impossible for it not to. He had set in motion a gigantic steam-roller of effects and it drew nearer and nearer every minute. What would Anna – the poor, poor love – what would Anna do?

Sarah came home early. She passed her mother's friend Gillian on the way down the street and Gillian said, with that broad, fat smile Sarah so hated, "Hardly worth going to school these days, is it?" Sarah had smiled in return. It was not worth defending herself. Gillian disliked her. She disliked her clothes, her boy-friends, her whole style. One only had to look at Gillian's own daughter to know what Gillian liked: smooth, well brushed hair; rosy cheeks; no make-up; dirndl skirts; fresh, white blouses. But Sarah's blood regularly boiled. No retaliation was possible, that was what was so upsetting. Anna, her mother, would not allow it. She said Gillian, for all the bland, easy-going exterior, was easily hurt.

The house was empty, which made Sarah happy. Usually her mother was there, fussing about, waiting to be talked to, and it was very tiring responding when she had so much school-work to do. She looked on the table for a note – Anna had a passion for notes detailing all kinds of domestic information – but there was none. No ovens to be put on or off, no clothes to be brought in from the clothes-line, no bits of shopping to get. It was comforting to sit eating Penguin chocolate biscuits and drinking strong sugary tea without a lecture on how bad for her they both were.

She sat in the kitchen for over half an hour, day-dreaming. She was not a rebel, nor did she hate either her home or her parents. When others at school railed against the horrors of both she was silent. But one day she would put all this orderliness and cleanliness behind her and live in glorious disarray as she wished. It pained her to see the amount of effort Anna put into organising the house. Day after day she bustled about, bossing Lily, their cleaning lady, striving for a state of perfection which Sarah found revolting. The big moment of the day was when her father, Robert, opened the front door (brass knocker always shining) and said, "I'm home!" Then Anna kissed him on the cheek and they had a quick cuddle before he divested himself of his working suit.

Sarah washed her cup out. Imogen and Harry would be home soon. She wanted to be well clear of the kitchen before they arrived. Upstairs, thirty-eight stairs up, she was remote from the main life of the house. Gathering her bag, full of heavy books, she trailed slowly up the stairs, taking in the minute changes of the day as she went without consciously registering that she was doing so. The stair-carpet had been cleaned, there was a basket full of fresh laundry on the first half-landing, the plants outside the sitting room window had been watered and were very slightly dripping. As she passed her parents' bedroom she saw Anna's awful jeans – she was much too old for those frightful jeans – lying on the bed. Faint wafts of perfume eddied gently out of the room. Curious, Sarah paused. Usually Anna informed her of every boring engagement she was about to have but she had mentioned nothing about today. Wasn't it the day for her voluntary work at the hospital? It would be some dreary relative she had unexpectedly gone to meet – nothing more exciting than that.

She lay on her bed, soothed by the muddle cocooning her, now she was among her own things. Anna's life lacked any excitement at all. Nothing, so far as Sarah could see, ever happened to her mother and yet she was not unhappy. She had her house, her blessed girl-friends by whom she set such store (Sarah disliked friends of her own sex), her voluntary work at the hospital and of course her husband, Robert. Every day seemed gratifyingly full in a way which astonished Sarah, who felt she alone saw their emptiness. Anna was untrained, virtually uneducated. She had left school at eighteen, taken a shorthand and typing course, worked for four years in Gusset and Crowther and then married the divine, newly arrived, impecunious editorial assistant, Mr Robert Osgood. Since then she had been a Wife and Mother.

Sarah smiled lazily. The sun came through the glass on to her bed and she was dreadfully afraid that at three-thirty in the afternoon she was going to fall asleep. Last night she had not come in until one in the morning and she had felt tired all day. Being fucked by Tom was exhausting. They were in such a state of frenzy half the time and it left her drained and shaky. Often, she felt she could not get out of Tom's bed to go home, that she would have to succumb and fall asleep there and then, but she always managed to prod herself up and out into the cold night air. Tom did not always accompany her. He thought her mad to go at all, but, as Sarah repeatedly said, she had her family to consider. Tom's parents were divorced. He lived with his mother, who was much preoccupied with her own lover and did not care about Tom's morals. Tom simply did not understand what it was like to be the eldest child of happily married, loving parents.

He goaded her, often. "Do you *want* to be like them?" he would ask with an aggravating sneer. "All cosy and sub-urban, bed at eleven after the cocoa?"

"You know I don't," she would sigh, "but I have to respect it while I'm still with them."

"Why?"

"You wouldn't understand why."

She hardly understood herself. They were so vulnerable, her parents, Anna and Robert. They loved each other, they had never even looked at anyone else in their entire lives. It made her feel impatient just to think about it. They never seemed to get bored with each other, nor to quarrel, not seriously. She still sometimes found them locked in a clinch in some dark corner of the house and she would creep away, half appalled at the evidence of such apparent passion after twenty years of married life. It would never happen to her, she knew it would not. Already, at eighteen, she had had six lovers and showed no signs of settling down. None of them had meant a thing to her either – they were just ways of satisfying her own lust, of experimenting with sex. Until Tom the experiments had mostly been failures. Like everything else she had discovered the hard way that sex needed practice to make perfect. (And she did not consider love.)

Anna and Robert would deny that. Sarah sighed and settled more comfortably on top of her duvet. They had practised, presumably, with each other and it had all come out right in the end. Or had it? It *seemed* to have done. But what about now, when Anna was getting lined and plump and grey-haired? Could Robert overlook this unattractive aging? That was what puzzled Sarah. She could see why her parents, Anna and Robert, loved each other but what she could not see was how Robert could any longer *fancy* her mother. It was not a subject she could broach. If Robert really did truthfully still fancy Anna, if her father really did fancy her mother after an approximate million fucks, then he must be blind. Or was he afraid to fancy anyone else? Or did

he stick to Anna because there was no safe alternative? The
ors blended into each other and Sarah fell asleep.

Claire had been told not to telephone. On no account, not
even in an emergency so dire she could contemplate no other
course. Nor was she to write. Their sole communication was
through meetings, each arranged by Robert, who alone was
allowed to telephone. It seemed unfair and overdone but that
was how it had always been and Claire accepted it. Robert
broke out in a sweat at the thought of Anna finding out and
it would have been cruel to threaten to do so, or run any risk,
by trying to contact Robert, of her doing so. The rules were
firmly laid out and inflexible.

Robert loved Anna, that was clearly understood by
Claire. He *loved* her, adored her, thought she was wonderful,
could not do without her. He loved his children, especially
Imogen, and his home. They were precious to him and
Claire knew he would never under any circumstances
whatsoever leave them: wife, children, home – they were all
sacrosanct. He had always been open about this, right from
the beginning. And she did not mind. It quite amused her to
hear Robert wax so lyrical on the subject. She assured him,
truthfully, that she had no desire to threaten his domestic
bliss. She was not jealous of Anna. Indeed, she pitied her and
was as keen as Robert to protect her. She didn't want Robert
to divorce Anna – perish the thought – and marry her,
certainly not. She was quite happy that things should go on
just as they were. Alarmingly, it was Robert who was not.

Claire sat with the manuscript of a book on ocean-going
liners on her desk, copy-editing it for the proof stage. Her
pencil wavered over one incomprehensible word and she
sought a dictionary. Her spelling was weak. She only liked
editing novels but James and James hardly published any
novels. She had been better off, much better off, at Gusset

and Crowther but apart from the Robert situation she wanted to leave that venerable firm to gain more experience. One day, she saw herself as starting a firm of her own, and she would publish new novels. Everyone she knew in the publishing world smiled wearily when she came out with this ambition and said it could never, ever be fulfilled – fiction was finished, the economic conditions made it impossible even to contemplate a publishing house existing only on new fiction – but Claire was not deterred. She was young (twenty-two) and obscenely ambitious.

Robert had been no part of her ambitions. She had wanted nothing of him originally except his occasional company and, afterwards, bed. She had never wanted him to live with her, still didn't, was a little horrified when he wistfully spoke of this being forever impossible. He was a lovely man, handsome and dynamic, they had a lot in common and their love-making was sublime. But quite often – *quite often* – Claire found herself glad when Robert had gone home to Anna. She simply liked to be on her own, to get on with her work, to read, to do just what she liked, even if what she liked amounted to no more than taking a bath and washing her hair. (She could do both those things when Robert was there but then they seemed necessary tasks, not pleasures.) It was Robert who fretted about the future and this state of affairs being purgatory; she did not. When pushed by Robert to say how she thought they could go on like this she said perfectly well, thank you.

Robert's decision was madness. She did not understand it. He had not consulted her, just told her, white-faced, of what he had so foolishly done. Now it was too late to persuade him not to be so silly. She had said she was going to ignore it. She looked at the green telephone on her desk and hoped it would *not* ring. It could only bring complications, which she hated. If Robert never rang or wrote or appeared in her life again she would be very sad – she expected she might even cry a little – but might she not also be relieved? Surely Robert had begun to interfere with her peace of mind, to get in the way of her work? She did not know if she could handle him any more. It annoyed her to remember his stricken look when she had said he could not come and live with her in her flat. She just did not want him there on any sort of day-to-day basis. He could come every day, oh yes, but she didn't want him to officially live with her. He would have to get his own place if he was leaving home.

The boring, boring book finished, Claire got up to go out. She didn't have lunch but she enjoyed walking around Covent Garden. One of the blessings of Robert being in Wandsworth was the impossibility of her reverie being spoiled by meeting him. She could saunter around, her own person. That was how she liked it. Now Robert had carried through his insane plan, his wife Anna would at this moment be imagining her as a scheming hussy, a marriage-breaker, a rival determined to wrestle the beloved Robert away. That was what she would think, wasn't it?

Two

Wandsworth High Street held quite a lot of attraction for Betty Munroe, though she naturally hardly dared to say so in front of Robert. She could cope with the shops there, didn't mind what Robert called their appalling ugliness one little bit. In fact, they suited her, she felt comfortable within them, far more comfortable than she had done in Soho Square – not that there were any actual shops there, next to the old offices, but it was only a few yards to Oxford Street and that was where Betty had spent her lunch-hours. It was one of the reasons she had taken the Gusset and Crowther job in the first place. It had excited her to think of the Oxford Street shops, of Peter Robinson's and D. H. Evans and, at the end, Selfridges. The excitement had soon passed. Her lunch-hours had become a torment and at the end of each one she had had a headache and felt utterly miserable. It was the amount of stuff in the shops which confused and sickened her. She might want to buy a skirt and she would go into

Peter Robinson and there would be hundreds and hundreds of skirts and her head would start to ache. In Wandsworth High Street there were no problems. There were two or three shops which might have a likely skirt and Betty could be in and out of them in five minutes, perfectly calm.

She even felt superior in Wandsworth High Street, a feeling very rare for Betty. She had begun working at Gusset and Crowther four years ago as a temporary and she had thought instantly it was not her kind of place, not her kind of people. There was no Mr Gusset but Mr Crowther was very much in evidence and Betty felt he despised her. She hated taking his dictation. He had a habit of making sarcastic personal remarks – "Ah! The mini-skirt returns, Miss Munroe, or have we had an accident?" He stressed the "Miss" and looked at her knees and she didn't know what he meant anyway. He was a large, shapeless man who wore loud checked suits like a bookie and prowled ponderously up and down the narrow staircases of the three-storey building. If Betty met him there was no way she could get past.

Nor was she happy with the other members of the Gusset and Crowther hierarchy. They all seemed to exclude her while appearing friendly. The women were university graduates working for tuppence but looking as though they were millionaires (or so she felt), and none of them ever chatted in the ladies or in the little kitchen in the basement as Betty wanted to chat. They smiled at her, always, and were ostentatiously considerate and it was not what Betty wanted at all. She had been more at home working for an executive at Nestlé's headquarters.

But when Mr Crowther asked her to stay she agreed, to her own surprise. She agreed, in spite of the relatively low pay and boring office, because of Robert Osgood, whom she adored. Mr Crowther probably knew that. "You would be Mr Osgood's secretary, officially," he had said, "but occasionally I would – ah – use you." She had said yes extremely quickly to shut him up. There were no doubts in her mind that Robert Osgood was the most wonderful man in the world.

It was not his looks which Betty admired most, though he was unmistakably handsome. His height was unremarkable, perhaps just under six feet, and his physique not exactly spectacular but he had one of those open, square faces with regular features that women consider "rugged". His hair was a dull sort of brown, though it was thick and plentiful and pushed aside from his forehead in a satisfactorily careless way, and his eyes were very healthy. Betty had noticed this straight away – Robert had such *healthy* eyes. The whites were absolutely clear, not a broken blood-vessel anywhere, and the irises were a hard, sharp bluey-grey. You couldn't get past Robert's eyes, or Betty couldn't. He had nice teeth too, though Betty was privileged to know that the teeth were a bit of a mirage because she made his dental appointments and knew how much trouble he had with crowns and bridges and caps. But Robert's television advertisement looks were nothing: it was his personality Betty loved. He smiled a lot and he was witty. Betty often burst out laughing at the most inopportune moments – in a darkened room at the optician's, having her eyes tested – just thinking of something Robert said. He was full of energy, which Betty liked though she was a slow sort of person herself, and he was kind. On his desk was a lovely photograph of himself, his wife, his three children, all on bicycles in the country. Betty could look at it for hours and hours.

She had met Anna and the children, of course. She had been to Robert's home, on a Sunday, for lunch. He was that sort of employer. She had been terrified, spent hours and hours changing from one outfit to another beforehand, and the thought of being given something she didn't like to eat had filled her with anguish. Sunday lunch at home in

Dundee had been a noisy, slapdash affair – Mrs Munroe, who worked in the factory all week, resented making a traditional lunch at all and it showed – and she was unused to formal meals. She did not know, afterwards, whether she was disappointed or not that the Osgoods' Sunday lunch had not been formal. They all sat round a large wooden table in the kitchen and nobody stood on any ceremony. They didn't have a roast either. They had a steak and kidney pie and a green salad afterwards and then apple crumble and ice-cream. Robert sat at the head of the table and talked to Betty, on his right, all the time.

That had been three years ago and since then Betty had become familiar with the entire Osgood family. She had, she supposed, been a little surprised to find Robert's wife so very ordinary – she was quite pretty, quite bright, quite every-thing. Betty was much too intelligent herself to make the mistake of writing Anna Osgood off just because it emerged she also had only been a secretary but nevertheless Anna did lack presence. But Robert loved her dearly. Betty had never seen such a loving couple. She was proud of Robert for loving his rather humble wife so much, proud that he never looked at any other woman. They looked at him – Betty was in a position to see that – but he did not respond. He was faithful. Instead of his faithfulness depressing her, because it gave her no room for hope, it consoled her. In a strange way it made her freer to love Robert. He was unobtainable, untouchable and that was good and safe.

Out Betty stepped into Wandsworth High Street, intend-ing to have a sandwich and a glass of milk at the snack-bar on the corner, and who should she see but Robert's wife, Anna Osgood, getting out of her car. Betty stopped abruptly. Anna never came to the office. Sometimes, very occasionally indeed, she had come to the Soho office, but never to Wandsworth. Furthermore, Robert was not here, he was not in his room to greet Anna. After a morning of doing nothing at all and continuing to look grey and ill he had suddenly rushed out at noon without saying where he was going. Betty felt deeply perturbed. Anna could only have come because something had happened (but why had she not rung first?). Anna had seen her and was coming across the road to meet her. "Oh Anna," said Betty, "Robert is out – I don't know where he has gone – he looked awful – I was surprised you let him come in at all, very surprised."

"Betty," Anna said, smiling, "it's you I wanted to see. I want to take you out for lunch and talk to you."

Ignoring his car Robert took a bus to the Aldwych. It took forever getting there. He had plenty of time to stare out of the window and come to his senses but they remained absent. By the time he got off the bus and began walking he felt he would not be responsible for any of his own actions ever again. Everything distracted him. All his thought-patterns were jumbled up. Trying to read, this morning, words leaped out of the text which were not there – words like "traitor" and "bastard" and "cheat" – and then he would begin a defence against the word until the next one appeared. If only, at the root of this nightmare, there had been the plain, stark fact that he no longer loved Anna. But there was not. He did love Anna. He loved his marriage. He could not bear to think of not going home every night to Anna and Sarah and Imogen and Harry. Without them he would cease to function. They were all part of him. They were what he had always wanted and prayed he would be lucky enough to get. He had been a family man before he was a man, always worried that he would not be able to create a unit like the unit into which he himself had been born. "Being tied down" was a phrase used by his contemporaries which he did not understand. At Oxford, friends had talked gloomily of the future, envisaging marriage and "being tied down" with dread, and he had tried to join in and to hide his own disappointment that he still, at twenty-one, had not met and fallen in love with any girl with whom he would willingly be tied down.

Then he went to London and started working at Gusset and Crowther and he met Anna. It was a deep, internal passion. Their eyes met and there it was – the connection, the sense of unity he had been looking for. But he had not rushed into anything. He took her out many, many times before he asked her home for the weekend and it was a whole year before they slept together. By then he had no doubts at all. His mother had – "She isn't somehow your match, Robert," – but he had none. Anna *was* his match. What his mother meant was that she was not an intellectual, which she fondly believed him to be. If Anna had been to university and had been in a profession there would have been no talk of her not being his match. What his mother (and others, rather too many others) did not realise was that Anna could have gone to university. She was perfectly clever enough. But two older sisters had given her a chip on her shoulder by being much, much cleverer and she had resolved to rebel against following in their footsteps. Anna's cleverness was a secret in which Robert revelled. Only he knew how critically astute she was, how sharp, how well read. To the world she perversely chose to present another image.

So he loved Anna. Twenty years had not altered his mind. Things had changed, both in obvious and subtle ways things had changed between them, but the love was still there. Even the sex was still there, though not so often and not so exciting. If sex had become a routine comfort, merely a warmth in the bed, Robert, who was a very truthful man, might have wondered about the quality of his love these days, but it had not. Quite often he was startled by the experience making love with Anna could still be. Not every night. Not every week. Not at any particular time or in any particular pattern but often enough to rate as not an exception. It was extraordinary and precious and he knew that for the whole of the next day after such a coupling he always looked shifty, as though he had something to hide which he preferred others not to know.

In Covent Garden Robert crossed the new open concourse and made for the shops he knew Claire liked to browse around. It was wrong of him to set out to catch her unexpectedly – she did not like it – but he felt a great need simply to look at her. He loved Claire. He experienced the same sense of connection as he did with Anna. When first he had acknowledged this he had been panic-stricken – he had fought against the truth, dismissed it as physical attraction and nothing more. Certainly, Claire *was* attractive, much more so than Anna had ever been. She was tall, had beautiful legs, long black hair and an athletic, shapely body. There was something dramatic about her which compelled attention. And of course with a First in English from University College, London she was undeniably brilliant. She would go places. Already, people were jealous and a little afraid of her. They said of her (as they had once said of Robert) that publishing was not her medium. She would be better off in television or journalism where her looks and self-confidence would be more of an asset. Publishing was a behind-the-scenes job, unsuited to those hungry for measurable success and adulation. It annoyed them that Claire seemed impervious to her own unsuitability.

Claire had always said he could have his cake and eat it. She, after all, had seduced him and was proud of it. She had made all the running and had not been put off by his agonising. Nor had all the difficulties in the way of their affair disheartened her. Together at last, she had laughed long and loud at the end of the chase. It had exhilarated her.

"Well, of course it was deliberate," she had laughed. "Of course I decided to have you. Robert, you must *know* how attractive you are? And your virtue makes you irresistible."

He had been so upset. "You make me feel cheap," he had said.

"You weren't cheap, you were very, very expensive – an enormous investment of precious time. All that extra reading just to impress you, Robert, all that trailing in your conscientious wake so that I would register at all. Then dealing with your prudery – I thought you would pass out when I asked you for a lift to Leeds that time. You were so very, very hard to seduce."

"Don't, Claire," he had said, "I don't like it. I don't like to think this was engineered."

"But Robert, how could you think it was anything else?"

"I thought we just fell in love," he said, embarrassed.

"Love, Robert? Nobody said anything about love." And then she had whispered in his ear, "Yes, I do love you, Robert dear, don't listen to me."

From then onwards she had made it all very easy. He went to her flat whenever he wanted to – she never sought him out nor complained if he did not come for weeks. They went away to Frankfurt together, to the Booksellers Conference, and to Leeds again for a *Yorkshire Post* dinner where an author of Robert's was getting a prize. They met surprisingly often at different functions. Nobody guessed what was going on because Robert's reputation was unsullied. They had good times together without arguments or strain and the affair could have gone on forever, or until Anna found out. That, Robert had concluded at the end of nights and nights of debate, was at the heart of his decision. He could not stand this deceit.

He could not see Claire anywhere. Either he was too late

or too early or she had not come today. Without thinking, Robert set off walking, not in the direction of Wandsworth but northwards, towards Highgate and home. His key was still in his pocket. If he could not see Claire he must have something to settle him. Anna would not be in at this time. It was her afternoon pushing the library trolley round at the hospital. He would go home, just for an hour.

Anna took Betty to the wine bar in the High Street. They settled themselves in the corner with a carafe of the house red and some French bread and cheese. It was rather dark and gloomy in their corner – Anna said no, she did not want a lamp put on, nor candles lit – and Betty could not help feeling a *frisson* of excitement. She drank half a glass of wine and waited, already a little light-headed and the better for it.

"Betty, how long have you worked for Robert?"

"Four years."

"It's a long time, long enough to know him very well, I should think."

"Oh yes, I *do* know him well. Of course, not as well as *you* do," Betty added hurriedly. She had perhaps spoken too confidently.

"We've been married twenty years."

"Yes, I know. Your anniversary was in April. Robert bought you a ring, didn't he?"

Wordlessly, Anna extended her hand. She had nice hands, the skin honey-coloured, the nails faintly pink and healthy looking. The sapphire, in a silver setting, was on the finger next to her wedding ring.

"Beautiful," Betty murmured, and drank some more wine. Her intuition was working overtime and she was becoming seriously alarmed.

"Rings – presents – don't mean much," Anna was saying. "I've never thought they were important. Nice to have, but it wouldn't upset me if Robert never bought me anything. I don't need presents. Not from Robert. I know he loves me. That's enough."

"Of course you do. He's devoted. Everyone knows."

There was a pause. Betty crumbled her bread desperately. She prayed to be delivered safely from the test ahead. It seemed to her obvious that Anna had come to confess that she was leaving Robert — it could be nothing else. He had been so distraught lately. Clearly, he had suspected something. With lightning speed, Betty readjusted her image of Anna. She ought always to have known. Now, looking at her, Betty saw how cheap Anna was. Especially since she had cut her hair. It made her look so butch, so very unfeminine, and it also made her look fatter and squat. Betty saw how her skin had coarsened lately and her complexion faded. She was just no match for Robert, especially not in that awful green dress. Robert was still youthful, he got better-looking all the time, but looking at Anna one saw how unkindly middle age was treating her. Instead of feeling sympathetic Betty felt a little contemptuous. If *she* had been Robert's wife she would have taken more care of herself, lived up to him. After all, Anna was not short of money. She could have her hair done weekly. She could have her face done. She could buy as many clothes as she liked. There was really no *need* for her to look so excessively dowdy and frumpy. She could slim, she could keep fit, she could try, for goodness sake. To think a woman like this was leaving a man like Robert, and for whom? Some disgusting, equally fat sweaty oaf, doubtless. Vulgar. The more you looked at her the more you saw it. No wonder she was white, no wonder her hand was shaking. The bitch. Betty took a very deep breath and resolved she would say exactly what she thought.

"Betty, you post Robert's letters, don't you?"

"Of course."

"Personally?"

"Yes. On my way home."

"Do you ever look at them – at the addresses – as you're putting the stamps on – as you're popping them in the postbox?"

"Yes. I do. I like to make sure I've typed them properly."

"Did you cast your eye over them last night?"

"Yes."

"Was there one addressed to me?"

Betty stared at Anna, a tightening round her heart. There had been one for Anna, she remembered it vividly. Why had it not struck her as strange that Robert should give her a letter to post to his own wife, to whom he returned every night? She had thought nothing of it. But there had been no letter, she was sure – not that she herself had typed. She would have remembered that.

"Yes, there was," she said, "but I didn't type anything to you. Robert must have written the letter himself and typed the envelope."

"Yes, he did. That's exactly what he did."

"Well, it isn't any of my business –"

"Betty, you love Robert, don't you? Oh, I'm not accusing you of anything horrid – I know *how* you love him. You wouldn't like to see him unhappy, would you? His life in ruins? His children his enemies? His home closed to him?"

"Whatever are you saying, Mrs Osgood?"

"I want you not to have posted that letter, Betty. For Robert's sake. Will you promise me that you didn't post it?"

"But I did."

"No, you didn't. I didn't receive it, so you didn't post it. When Robert asks you – if he asks you – you dropped all those letters into the incinerator and you had to type them all again. All except the one to me because you had no black of it. So I couldn't have got any letter."

"We haven't got an incinerator –"

"You'll think of something."

"– and I would never be so careless. Robert wouldn't believe such a silly story."

"He will believe anything today. He will probably cry with relief or faint when you tell him. I shouldn't be surprised if he kisses you, he will be so glad."

Anna now drank some of her own wine for the first time. She could see Betty was mesmerised – everything was going to be all right, just as she had known it would be. There was no need to worry. She had kept her wits about her and moved fast. Now she must go on from this first victory and consolidate her success. She smiled brilliantly at poor little Betty – a sweet, homely, common girl who was so naïve as to be almost simple-minded. There was only one thing more she wanted of Betty.

"Betty," she said, whispering, "when Robert goes away you book his hotels, don't you?"

"Yes."

"Where did he stay last night?"

"I didn't book a hotel for last night. He was in London, at home."

"Thank you, Betty. So he was."

Robert let himself in very quietly. He knew the children would be home soon, that there was not much time. It felt strange to be opening the front door and not shouting "I'm home!" The hall was full of sunshine, bouncing off the red and blue stained glass panels of the door. He rarely saw it like that. Usually, the hall was a dull place by the evening, somewhere to rush through and that was all. But now, though he did not have time, he lingered, peering into the mirror above the long shelf that was cluttered with keys and stamps and gloves and bags. He felt like a burglar, caught unawares by his own image and scared by it because he had thought nobody was in.

The kettle was still hot. He put his hand on its shining side and pondered the significance of this. Hot, just used, at three o'clock in the afternoon with Anna out since one and the children not due until four. Kettles must retain their heat a long time. He re-boiled it and made himself some coffee. There was more sun in the kitchen, stroking the pinewood walls and surfaces. Pinewood since 1972, when the extension was built. Slowly, he walked, coffee cup in hand, the length of the kitchen and the living room, where plants quietly waved in the infinitesimal breezes which invisibly stir them. The piano, Imogen's piano, rented at first, bought after she passed Grade 4. It was newly polished, the dark wood gleaming, but the keys seemed dirty. There was a treadle sewing machine in the other alcove, still used, a bright red bobbin threaded in and bunched-up red pattern material lying across it. Then there were the books, all one wall, floor to ceiling in alphabetical order, and a huge trestle table covered in papers. Cushions, a sofa, several chairs, rugs – he remembered them all. Only yesterday since he had seen them yet he remembered them all.

He played a game. Starting at the door, he tried to go round this battered family room and identify where everything had come from, where it had been bought, at what stage in their married life it had been acquired. There had been jumble sales, Camden Passage antique shops, country sales (accounting for all the stripped pine bits), Habitat, John Lewis, Aunt Jessica's stuff, rugs from Casa Pupo. He could hardly remember any prices, unless at the time they had broken the bank. He stuck over an early Victorian sewing table – where? when? how much? Anna would know. Everything was precious to her. The accumulation of belongings so important. Once accumulated, they had become precious to him too. On their own they were nothing, he would not miss them, but together, arranged as they were, together he needed them.

"Dad?"

He jumped, went to the foot of the stairs.

"Sarah? What are you doing home?"

"Got out early. We didn't go to the Courtauld after all. Where's Mum?"

"It's her afternoon at the hospital, isn't it?"

"Oh yeh. Funny."

"What?"

"I thought I smelled her posh outing perfume in the bedroom. And she's taken her jeans off."

She was down now, going past him into the kitchen. Not at all like her mother, Anna. Like him, no doubt about it. He watched her covertly, imagining her reaction to what he had done. Anna could not have told her. Of course not – he would not have expected her to. She would be brave.

"Where were you last night?" Sarah asked, yawning. He noticed how white her teeth were, God knew how since she never brushed them. She wore this startlingly red lipstick at the moment which made her mouth look savage.

"Oh – away," he said. The mechanics of lying eluded him. He was going to be hopeless in the months that followed.

"You're home early too," Sarah said, he thought accusingly. "Don't you feel well? You don't look well."

"No, I don't, do I? I just felt like a walk home."

"A walk? Where from? Not Wandsworth?"

"No. Covent Garden."

"Dad, I think you're going bonkers."

He drifted round the kitchen, ended up playing with the cord of the window-blind.

"Sarah, when did you last see your mother?"

She burst out laughing. He smiled weakly. "I mean, have you seen her today?"

"No. But she was here. You needn't think she's run away. I shouted hello on my way to the front door and goodbye when I got to it and she shouted back. Why?"

"I just wondered." The overwhelming urge to confide in Sarah was growing in him. She was a girl of the world. Those youths with whom she consorted certainly weren't interested in just holding her hand. It might be better if he told her his marriage was in peril, the marriage between her parents.

"Sarah," he began.

Anna drove back to town, steadily, carefully, paying great attention to traffic-lights. Now she *was* nervous. Betty was one thing, Claire another. Her heart raced at the thought of confronting Claire, a girl half her age whom she hardly knew. She had seen her twice, at parties, and though she had not thought her beautiful she could see that she was attractive and impressive. She had charm too. Anna was used to being either snubbed or despised at literary parties. She wasn't anyone, only there on Robert's coat tails. Sometimes she would try to start a conversation over a novel she had just read but people went glazed – her opinion was nothing to them. Claire Bayley had appeared to care about her opinion. She had invited it, on the merits of that year's winner of the Booker Prize, and she had listened while Anna gave it and responded. There had been nothing arrogant about her.

Parking in Covent Garden would not be easy. Anna had made an appointment, without giving her real name, for two-thirty. If she failed to find a parking place she would just stop straight outside the James and James offices and get fined or towed away. But she did find a place, in Henrietta Street, and she had time to spare. She would walk once round the block and then go in, regardless. Unfortunately, the heel of her new shoes caught in a grating and not only did she wrench her ankle badly, the heel snapped off. She stood holding her shoe in her hand, knowing it was now unwearable. If it had been a flat shoe the difference would have been negligible but three inches down on one foot was a long way to go. There were no shoe shops in Henrietta Street. Scrambling in her bag, Anna found the end of a roll of Sellotape. Crouching in the gutter, she tied the heel on, wrapping the Sellotape right round her ankle. The nails, tiny nails, were still in the base of the heel and the strapping-up might hammer them in.

She presented herself at the reception desk. "I have an appointment with Miss Bayley," she said, clutching onto the side of the window through which a haughty young lady eyed her. "The name is Grey."

"Will you hold on?" the girl said.

"Yes."

"Miss Bayley, I have your two-thirty appointment here. Thank you."

A buzzer sounded. "Go right on up," the girl said, staring in such an unfriendly way. Anna nodded graciously and limped up the stairs. She had meant to be a threatening figure, menacing even, powerful, thunderously self-righteous. She was going to lay down the law in no uncertain terms, just as she had done to Gillian and Lucy.

The office inhabited by Claire Bayley was small. Anna was grateful. In no time at all she was seated, the hideous shoe hidden. She sat very straight-backed, on the edge of the seat, to make up for not standing. It was disconcerting that Claire had not seemed surprised, only welcomed her courteously and never even mentioned the assumed name. But Claire *was* surprised. The flushed face of Anna Osgood told its own tale. Rapidly, Claire ran over the alternatives before her. She could lie and pretend she did not know what Anna had come for. She could take the lie further and pretend she did not know what Robert had done. She could move on to swear she did not want to break Anna's marriage. But what she would not do was give up Robert if he did not wish to give up her.

"I'm sorry to burst in on you like this," Anna said, "so deceitfully. I thought you might not see me if I gave my real name."

"Oh, I would have done. But I would probably have suggested my flat or lunch or something."

"Yes, I'm sorry to come to your office too, but I don't know where you live and I thought an office atmosphere might be best. I want to be businesslike, pet."

Anna blushed deeply. The pet had slipped out. Her mother had called her pet in moments of great emotion and she had always called Robert pet as a joke.

"I'm sorry. I *do* want to be businesslike."

"About what?"

"Robert. My husband. You aren't going to pretend there is nothing between you, are you?"

"No."

"Well then, I want to discuss the situation rationally, without getting upset."

"Good. Would you like some coffee?"

"Yes."

She should not have said yes. It meant waiting, her inside churning, watching Claire boil the electric kettle set up on a small table in the corner. Her dark hair fell forward across her fine-boned face and she pushed it back with a casual gesture. Anna was distressed to find this emphasised Claire's youth. She hadn't seemed young to talk to but now, as she made the coffee, all her movements seemed young.

But she was glad to hold the hot mug. The warmth was

immensely soothing. She cleared her throat. "I received a letter from Robert this morning. I expect you know about it?"

"He told me he would write. I begged him not to."

"Why?"

"I think he's being silly."

The coffee was more necessary than ever. One, two, three gulps. Dreadful complications loomed ahead.

"He should be brought to his senses, don't you think?" Claire was saying. "I think it's up to you to sort him out, don't you?"

Three

Sarah cut chocolate cake in Gillian's kitchen – thick, gooey slices, all running with double whipped cream. It was one of the perks of babysitting for Gillian, and Sarah availed herself of what was available without compunction. The cake made up for the coldness of the house and changing the baby's filthy nappy twice and putting up with a lot of lip from the other two daughters.

Settled in front of the television, watching some rubbish – she was just deliberately going to slump and watch any old thing – Sarah munched steadily, eyes on the screen, thinking. It was a wonder it had not happened before but she had been unable to get her dad to see this. What was abnormal was his belief that he was abnormal just because, at last, he had a bit on the side. His anguish was really embarrassing. She had hardly been able to look at him as he sat with his head in his hands mumbling away, saying he deserved her contempt. It was bloody ridiculous. He was making himself ill over nothing. And then he had told her about the letter.

It was part of her dad's other-worldliness, Sarah reflected, that he should choose to write a letter spilling the beans. People thought he was dynamic but he was a dreamer. He might rush around snapping his fingers, all go, but inside he drifted hopelessly. She had always known it. That was her mother's power over him. Anna was practical. She dealt with life for Robert. She organised him. All the energy flowed from her to him, a one-way current. And now the fool had buggered up the works.

Of course, it could not be allowed to happen. There was no *need* for it to happen. She had tried to make him see that all he needed to do was apologise, say he would never see this Claire again, forget the whole thing. "I can't," he had said, "I can't give her up." She had explained he only needed to *say* he was giving her up, but he had groaned and shaken his head. Really, what a mess. Sarah felt even more angry in retrospect than she had done at the time. Robert was so infantile, so inept. He seemed to have no conception of how to behave. He was gauche. There he sat, a perfectly happy marriage around him, an affair in progress, nobody any the wiser and he threw it all away. He didn't seem to understand what people thought marriage was.

It was creepy too, the vision of Robert with this girl. Though she had been inquisitive, had pressed him, he had given nothing away except that she was twenty-two, beautiful, clever, very *nice*. Sarah laughed, spluttering cake crumbs everywhere, very *nice*. Well, Robert was nice too. He was good looking, attractive, far more so than poor old Mum. It had always been perfectly possible to imagine Dad in bed, rather dreadful to imagine Mum. And now, these days, Anna had nobody lusting after her. Anna, Gillian, Lucy, Elizabeth – oh dear, it was unkind, but none of them had any appeal. They had all been married ten, fifteen, twenty years.

It was what marriage – their sorts of marriage – did to you. A fate she, Sarah, would take care to avoid.

At nine, Tom came. A quick ping on the bell. Sarah took her time answering. She had a recurring vision of Gillian and her awful bald-headed husband, Doug, coming home early and finding Tom and her at it – she almost wanted it to happen, just to be off-hand, even with no clothes on. Gillian certainly suspected her. "There's a funny smell," she would say. Smoothly, Sarah would agree, adding, in a Gillian way, "I noticed it as soon as I came into the room but I didn't like to say anything. I said to Cathy, before she went to bed, I said, Cathy, there's a funny smell." Gillian would then open a window in silence.

Of course, they weren't stupid enough to use any of the beds. Good heavens, no. The floor was perfectly acceptable, preferable. The wall-to-wall Axminster, dark red, absorbed any semen effortlessly. A little stickiness, when dried out, was quickly rubbed in with the heel of a boot. Sarah wondered why they didn't feature this important attribute in advertisements. Rolling over and over did the carpet no harm either. Once, when the revolting baby woke, it had amused the creature no end to watch this violent activity. Sarah, interrupted mid-coitus, had thrust the infant (eight months) into its plastic chair and returned to the frenzy. "She's been happy just sitting watching me," she had said to Gillian. "Oh, you are good to have amused her." She got an extra quid.

"I can't concentrate tonight," Sarah said. "I'm worried."

"Oh yeah?"

"It's my dad. He's told my mum he's got a mistress."

"You're joking. Well, bloody hell, what a laugh – after all you've said – all this crap about the saintly Robert –"

"He is saintly."

"Not if he's getting his leg over like anyone else. I told

you, didn't I? Didn't I say, I bet he's not perfect?"

"He is perfect. He's going mad. He's all to pieces – you should see him."

"Who's the girl?"

"Somebody who used to work with him. Young."

"Not the neighbours then. That's something to be thankful for."

"The thing is, he's told my mum."

"Did she go spare? I bet she bawled. Or fainted. Must've been a shock though."

"I don't know. I haven't seen her today. I've only seen him. He wrote her a letter."

"The daft bugger."

"I know. I can't think what to do."

"Is he shacking up with this girl?"

"No. He says he's going to live on his own."

"What's the point in that?"

"She doesn't want him living with her."

"He's a bloody loony. Why didn't he just carry on normally?"

"He says his marriage wouldn't allow it. He has to tell the truth or he couldn't live with himself."

"Jesus. Well. Nothing you can do."

"There is."

"Like what?"

"Well, I can't let it happen, can I? I can't just let him wreck his marriage."

"What's so marvellous about it? It's wrecked now anyway. Just like everyone else's."

"No, it isn't. It isn't at all like anyone else's. Robert and Anna, Dad and Mum, they're different. This affair is nothing, it isn't important. What they've got has to go on. You just don't give up a marriage like that."

"None of your business."

"Everyone says that. The children aren't supposed to do anything, are they? Nope. Just stand on the side-lines and pick up the pieces. Not me. I'm in the middle of it."

"You want to stay out of it." Tom yawned. For them, it had been a long conversation. "Could work to your advantage, in the end. Life would be a bit free and easier, like it is for me. You wouldn't have to feel so screwed up."

"I suppose," Sarah said, "I could go and see the girl, this person." The decision cleared her head. She began to take her clothes off.

Anna was back in time for Imogen and Harry coming home. She went up to her bedroom and took off her dress and put back on her jeans and shirt. Claire had been wearing jeans and a shirt. She felt very tired and very miserable. The fight seemed to have left her. It was a moment when she knew she had been right to tear Robert's letter into tiny pieces and flush it down the lavatory. Otherwise, she would have read it, over and over again, always at her most vulnerable. As it was, she was grateful to find rage and horror had so clouded her memory that she could think of only a few phrases.

There was a note from Sarah, off babysitting very early, not back until after eleven. Listlessly, Anna began to prepare supper. It was as though, that morning, she had been given a powerful shot of some stimulant and now it was wearing off. She felt only sick and shaky. She doubted her ability to dissemble. But when Imogen arrived home, Anna smiled and chatted, just as usual. Imogen, at twelve, looked eight. Totally unlike Sarah, she was frail and childlike and heavily protected by all her family ever since, two years ago, she had been in a car accident. Nothing damaged permanently, only her spleen removed, but nobody needed to be told the accident had left deep scars. Looking at Imogen hurt. One wondered whether she would last the day. She was wistful and withdrawn and had lost the secret of smiling. The doctor – the psychiatrist – said it would pass. It might take years, but it would pass. Luckily, he said, Imogen had one priceless asset: she was part of a settled, loving, stable family.

Harry's boisterous arrival was welcome. Large, untidy, clumsy and noisy fourteen-year-old Harry was a great trial to his sisters. He had many friends, equally large and noisy, who tended to congregate in the Osgood kitchen in the evenings. There, they played cards and laughed raucously, or watched television and surreptitiously smoked. Lately, Harry had taken to looking in mirrors and cutting his hair with pinking shears. He looked now as if he had ringworm. The girls made cutting remarks but Anna shushed them and said he was Growing Up and must be treated kindly.

Anna watched them eat. There had been a time when she had thought that without Robert she would die. He had only to go away for a night when they were first married and she had been desolate. The blankness of her busy day had terrified her. But then she had reached a stage – impossible to pin-point – when she had realised she would not die. She would not even want to die. The loss would be irreparable but she would not be left with nothing. The children, once they had grown up, would give her a life. Indeed, she had felt guilty thinking she would quite like that life, and immediately she had taken this back as though it had been walking across her own grave. The house, the children, without Robert, were shells, perfectly formed on the outside but empty and fragile.

Sarah would be all right, whatever happened after today. She was resilient and tough. Anyway, her childhood was over. She would be off to some university in October. But Imogen. . . And Harry, caught Growing Up. . . . Would they pity her, despise Robert? Would it bring out a tenderness in them, up to now hidden? Would they just carry on as usual, hardly noticing? They had never been tested. They might turn on her, blame her. They might accuse her of becoming an old slag, a shrew, a middle-aged empty-headed busybody, enough to drive any man away.

"Lucy wants to borrow some sugar," Imogen said. Lucy followed her into the kitchen. Sprightly Lucy in her flowered dress, that hair still flowing freely down her back at forty plus, bare legs (rather thick and defiantly hairy) slipped into strong sandals. Lucy of the good figure and cheerful temperament, an undowntrodden mother, passionately involved with her brood, married to slow, gormless Clive who had so magnanimously forgiven Lucy her little escapade. Now they were more Happily Married than ever – another baby to show for it – but Lucy's eye wandered. Certainly, it had wandered over Robert. Often. Any encounter between them and Lucy was the complete coquette. She believed all men fancied her. Once, in Gillian's kitchen, she had said so. "I know it sounds conceited but I just know – men *do* fancy me – I can read bed in all their eyes. I'm not saying they *would* all take me to bed if they could but I know they would like to." Anna remembered saying, coldly, that perhaps Lucy was using these tell-tale eyes as mirrors. Perhaps they reflected her own desire? She had asked Robert if he did fancy Lucy. No. She was, said Robert, messy. There was something messy about Lucy in every way and he hated messy women.

"Some sugar," Lucy said, beaming. "God knows how I forgot to get any. You're looking tired, Anna?"

"Mm. I am tired. It's been a busy day."

"Robert home yet?"

"No. Much too early for him."

"Of course, you always know exactly when he will come in. Lucky you. Clive is never home the same time two days running. Still, it means he can't complain if the supper isn't ready, doesn't it?"

Supper was never ready for Clive anyway, not in Lucy's house. Mostly, it was well known, he made it himself, poor sod. Lucy did not put him first. It was no part of their marriage that husbands should be welcomed home to a clean house and a good meal and an attentive wife. Lucy had not needed the help of Women's Lib. It was already in operation. She had an au pair girl, a cleaning lady, three of her children at school all day, but it was quite common for Clive to go out immediately once he had come home from work to shop for the supper. Then he would cook it, bath the baby and wash up. But Robert said it was wrong to judge other marriages by their own.

By seven o'clock Anna was standing at the window of the upstairs sitting room, watching. She could not help it. She stood half shrouded in the green silk curtain, staring over the window box down into the street. At any moment, Robert might turn the corner and then everything would be all right. The hardest part might begin but she would feel new courage. Tears came into her eyes as she thought of kissing Robert good evening — it was all she wanted, his *presence*. Was that too much to ask?

Betty found it very difficult to work at all that afternoon. She should not have had any wine. It did not agree with her without food and she had been too distraught to eat anything at all. The world was going mad. She felt it spinning before her eyes. Nothing had been clearly said. She went over and over the conversation with Anna and none of it made sense. She had been expected to pick things up and cotton on and she might have got it all wrong, quite wrong. Now that it was too late she realised she should have asked for some final clarification.

The gist was — surely it was — that Robert had written Anna a letter with something in it which Anna did not wish to know. The further gist was that he was having an affair with another woman and had left home. Or was it? It was the second bit that confused. What further upset Betty was the insult to her own surveillance. Could Robert be having an affair without her knowing?

Well, it was irrelevant. What mattered – tenth typing mistake in ten minutes – was whether she was going to do as Anna asked. Was it her place to intervene? There swam into her muddled head a picture of Robert and his family at Sunday lunch. She loved that picture. It was her ideal, one she was beginning to think she would never achieve. She would be wretched if the picture was spoiled. She needed it, to encourage her, console her. It was a sort of religion, Robert and Anna's marriage, and she was its most fervent convert.

Nothing very awful could happen if she pretended not to have posted the letter anyway. If Robert wanted to, he could just write it again, as simple as that. He could write it and make sure he posted it himself, or better still he could go and deliver it himself. It would merely give him a second chance, that was all. Perhaps he had acted hurriedly, perhaps his apparent ill-health had been a sign of remorse. Betty made up her mind: she would do what Anna had asked. In a dreadful fever of impatience she waited for Robert to return. Many ifs and buts occurred to her but the main outline of her duty was firmly drawn.

"Some milk," Lucy said, "if you could spare it – half a pint would do. Have you seen Anna today?"

"No," said Elizabeth. She omitted to add that she had seen nobody, nor was she likely to. The children – she only had two, seventeen and eighteen, hardly children – came home less and less. Apart from them, who would she see except people at work, with whom she had a strictly professional relationship imposed by her years ago and impossible to change now circumstances had changed? On her day off, Thursday, today, she saw no one. She took the dog for a walk and brooded magnificently. "No, I haven't. I haven't seen her for weeks. Our paths don't cross any more. They only ever did when the children were small and Jonathan was fond of Sarah."

"Hasn't she changed?" Lucy said, settling herself, quite unwanted, at the kitchen table with its brightly patterned PVC cloth.

Elizabeth's kitchen was perfectly clean and tidy but it always felt soulless, neglected. It was as though there had never been any light or noise in it, no jolly meals or companionship. And Elizabeth herself was so grave and tailored, both in clothes and looks. Her dark hair always beautifully coiled into a chignon, her pale oval face serene, her slight body quite fragile in matter-of-fact suits and dresses, she looked what she was: a professional woman running her life with efficiency and regularity. She hardly ever seemed to smile, she was what Lucy thought of as a "down" person, and it was always hard in her company not to go down with her. But she had sterling qualities too. She was truthful, reliable, not interested in forming alliances or grinding axes. She was above all that. In many ways she was above everybody.

"Who? Anna or Sarah?" Elizabeth asked.

"Sarah."

"I haven't seen her for weeks either."

"Oh, she's been changed for years, since she was fourteen. Remember how she used to look, when they were all at St Michael's? Such a pretty child – all that bubbly, curly hair and pink cheeks and always so neat and delicate looking. Now she's gross – she's fat and slovenly, her nose has got big and her mouth and her eyes are just slits –"

"Jonathan still seems to think she's attractive."

"Ah yes, but now it's sex, isn't it? It oozes out of her. I bet she's in and out of all their beds. I don't know how Robert and Anna put up with it."

"I don't suppose they have much choice. Your children are still young, Lucy."

"It's ironic, isn't it?" said Lucy, with extreme satisfaction. "Anna of all people having a daughter like that. I bet it makes her furious."

"No," said Elizabeth – oh, she did *not* like Lucy but Lucy alone visited her, gave her some semblance of company – "no, I don't think it would. It's more likely to make her sad. She'll wonder where she has gone wrong, if it's true, what you're saying, she'll feel guilty about it and look for reasons in how she's brought Sarah up."

"Strictly, that's for sure. Of course, Sarah's just reacting against the lovey-dovey scenario. Imagine *living* with Robert and Anna. It must be suffocating."

"I think they're wonderful."

"Oh, we all think they're wonderful. And unbelievable."

"I believe in them," said Elizabeth sharply. "I even believe there are plenty like them. Happy marriages – long-lasting ones – are still with us. Anyway, Lucy, I obviously don't want to go on with this subject. It hurts too much. I didn't have a happy marriage and now I haven't got an unhappy one either and I'm plain jealous."

"You're so honest, Elizabeth. I do admire you for it. I do wish you'd come round and see me sometime. Why don't you come for coffee, your next day off? Next Thursday? It isn't good for you never to see anyone. I'll ask Anna and Gillian too."

Elizabeth winced, but turned away to get the milk out of the fridge in time. Which would be more childish – to say she wanted to be alone or to express enthusiasm as though

47

she had been invited to a proper party? Either way she was humiliated and in any case she did not wish to go. Collectively, Lucy, Gillian and Anna bored her, always had done. As a professional woman (she was an accountant) kitchens full of women drinking coffee and chatting appalled her. She had only ever joined them to avoid seeming stand-offish. Their world was simply not her world, never had been, even when the children were small. But now she had no world. Work was a relief, not a world.

"Thank you," she said. "I'll try and pop in. But don't bother inviting anyone else – I'd really rather you didn't."

"Well, we'll see," Lucy said complacently. "We'll see who is around. You like Anna best, don't you?"

"I don't like anyone *best* that I know of."

"I've always thought you had most in common with her. I'll ask Anna. She's looking peaky."

"Oh?"

"Mm. I've just been in her house and I must say she didn't look her usual capable self. Not a smile, very drawn and tired-looking. I just wonder sometimes whether she is after all so happy. She says she is, everyone thinks she is, but sometimes I just wonder." Lucy traced a tiger-lily on the PVC. Elizabeth felt fury mounting in her. "She said some quite hard things about you the other week, you know."

"Thanks very much, Lucy. I don't want to know."

"Well, I think you ought to. I mean, I hate deceit, it really upsets me, it upsets Clive too. I think you ought to know Anna isn't what she seems. You think so highly of her, I know, but if you'd heard her the other day, saying she thought you were a coward and stupid and that you'd behaved absurdly – over Peter leaving you, you know –"

"Lucy, please. I must ask you to stop. I simply loathe people who go from one friend to another unloading poison."

"This isn't poison – it's the *truth*."

"The truth is often poisonous. It does me no good to hear what Anna Osgood thinks of me. Anyway, I don't care."

"She's too virtuous for words," Lucy said, ignoring, as she always did, any counter-riposte. "I suppose that's what irritates me about Anna. I know it's awful of me but sometimes I wish something terrible would happen to her –"

"Wasn't Imogen's accident terrible enough?"

"Yes, it was. But it didn't happen to Anna – oh, I know it affected her dreadfully and all that but it wasn't her fault. I meant something that would make her a bit more humble. If only she would fall in love with somebody or something."

"Like you did, you mean?"

"I didn't fall in love." Instead of resenting this reference, which Elizabeth had thought might be classed as snide, Lucy was delighted. Elizabeth had forgotten how she loved to talk about her fall from grace. Anna, Gillian and Elizabeth herself had all been told individually and sworn to secrecy. They all had had the tears and panic and recriminations and then the sly, sidelong looks of triumph from under Lucy's lashes. "I went to bed with Joe because I experienced overwhelming lust and he made advances and the house was empty and – well, you *know* it was lust. I never for one minute fell in love. I love Clive, that's why I married him. I'll always love him but I have to admit I do feel attracted to other men. That's all I want Anna to feel, so she knows what it's like."

"How do you know she doesn't?"

"She says she doesn't, publicly. She says she and Robert have only ever fancied each other."

"Well then, believe her."

"I do, that's what I'm saying – I wish she would fancy someone else, just to humanise her. Of course, she might be frigid. She never talks about her sex life."

"Thank God."

"No, but it's suspicious. If we're talking about orgasms or how many times we make love in a week she gets up and leaves. It's strange."

"I don't think it's strange. I think it's admirable."

"You're a puritan too."

"And frigid?"

"I didn't mean that. I know you aren't frigid."

"Because I went to bed with somebody apart from Peter? Your logic is a little at fault, Lucy. Anyway, I must go."

Lucy got up, reluctantly. She knew Elizabeth wasn't going anywhere and she felt aggrieved at being rebuffed. Clutching the milk, she said, "You won't tell Anna what I said, will you?" Hardly able to control her disgust, Elizabeth said, "I can't think of anything you said that is worth telling her."

"No, but you know what I mean — I don't really want anything awful to happen to her, not really — it was just —"

"Meanness? Jealousy?"

"Oh, I'm not jealous of Anna Osgood! I'd *hate* to be her. Good God, no. I only said what I said for fun really — just boredom with her as she is. It was harmless romancing — I was just amusing myself, the way one does?"

Lucy left, hating Elizabeth. She wasn't surprised Peter had left her. She was so cold, never responded in the right spirit. She ought to have known Elizabeth would not respond like Gillian, big, comfortable Gillian, who would have known exactly what she meant. Gillian, told that somebody was talking about her behind her back, would have cross-examined her and then gone round and confronted Anna. Lucy cheered up at the thought. Of course, Elizabeth would never do that. She was secretive, introverted. Good old Gillian would have waded in and such a lot of mischief would have ensued and then there would have been a final reconciliation and Lucy would have felt she had done some good exposing a friend's falseness. But Elizabeth could turn anything. Her coldness had made Lucy feel reprimanded. Instead of Elizabeth disliking Anna for speaking ill of her she had disliked Lucy. Everyone seemed to worship Anna Osgood, that was the trouble. She was holier-than-thou and as she returned home with sugar and milk Lucy wished her ill.

Robert took most of the afternoon getting back to his office in Wandsworth by bus and tube. He hated the journey at any time of the day but in the afternoon it seemed positively obscene. Outside, it was so beautiful – excepting the crowds and traffic and noise and buildings, he meant. His eyes were constantly drawn upwards to the blue sky and the trees – thank God London was a city of trees – and it felt like a further part of his madness not be out in the country where man had done nothing to defile the beauty of the elements.

And in the country there were no Claire Bayleys, no anybody that Robert could think of. If he had worked at home, in the country, nothing untoward would ever have happened. Proximity, opportunity – it was traitorous to Claire (perhaps even to Anna) to think how important they had been. He wondered, bitterly, why fate had decreed that Claire had come within his sphere but then he bravely rejected this way out of his guilt. Did he wish he had never set eyes on Claire? No. Well then. It was dangerous nonsense to entertain these romantic "if only" notions. There had been an act of will, never mind any other sort of more interesting act, and he had made it. Nothing got past that.

He hated the tube, hated the darkness and the smell and the ugliness. He hated the people too, all woeful and blank. On buses people were animated, they talked to each other. The buses were packed with the downtrodden and poor too but they did not seem the scum of the earth, as they did in the tube. He knew he had done a second wrong thing. First the letter, then telling Sarah. What had come over him? She had looked so assured, so made for bad news. But at the bottom of his base desire to tell her he knew there had been a wish to be chastised. He wanted his daughter to shout at him and hit him – he wanted to be made to defend himself. It was a practice for facing Anna, which at some point he would have to do. He wanted to see what a full frontal attack would do to his resolution. But Sarah had not attacked him. She seemed to find it difficult to comprehend that what he was confessing was horrifying. She had smiled with that glaring red mouth of hers, a superior, sardonic smile. Only when he had got on to writing to Anna had the smile disappeared. Then, she had indeed shown consternation but not of the kind Robert was looking for. She kept using words like "silly" and "foolish" and "unnecessary" when what he wanted was "cruel", "heart-breaking", "wicked". Especially "wicked". Sarah would not grant him wickedness even when he offered it to her. She grew irritable and said he must just carry on as usual. She was annoyed that he seemed to think any special course of action necessary. Once she had ascertained that he still loved Anna, that he still loved home and his marriage, she became more impatient.

It had been too much for an eighteen-year-old girl to understand. As he came up from the tube at Clapham and looked for a number 37 bus Robert realised this. He sweated at the thought of what disastrous consequences might have ensued from his revelations to Sarah – the shock could have been severe, worse even than for Anna. How lucky he therefore was that his daughter had been so unflustered. But he did not feel lucky. He felt let down. All the time he was expecting melodrama and getting a children's story. It occurred to him, for the first time, that perhaps life could just have gone on, as Claire had always said. What would have been wrong with it?

He closed his eyes as the bus trundled up Battersea Rise. Oh God. How many times he had analysed that one. It was not the moral wrongness of being unfaithful to his beloved wife which tormented him (though it did) but rather the wrong it did to him as a person. He could not go on being the same person. Loving Claire, wanting to be with her, just as much as with Anna, whom he also loved, changed him. He felt permanently fraudulent. This uncertainty had crept into every nook and cranny of his life and unmanned him. Yet when he had said to himself that the solution was to give up Claire he almost fainted with fright. That was a final solution, like death, and he did not want to die. The other alternative was to give up Anna and that was worse still. That was murder; the other, suicide. And so, by this painful process of elimination, he had thought of leaving his marriage – not Anna, not of leaving his wife, but of leaving his *marriage*, at least for a while. He would live on his own and visit Anna and Claire. He would put himself in this wretched position wilfully because he could not tolerate deception.

Sarah could not understand the distinction but then she had no experience of marriage. She didn't know what there was to leave, apart from people and a building. He had tried to explain that marriage was more. He had always seen his marriage as a living entity. It was made up of a myriad things – love, sex, companionship, security, stability, food, comfort, talk, worry, collective responsibility, sympathy, tenderness, criticism, support – all those and more. It grew all the time, fed on memories and shared, poignant experiences which nobody else could understand. There were always new discoveries to make, new perspectives to which one adjusted. It was the marriage that grew bigger and bigger while the members of it grew smaller and smaller. He now saw himself as very tiny indeed.

Last night – awful night – he had shut himself in that foul room, that brown and lifeless hotel bedroom, and waited for release to come. He quibbled with himself at his choice of word: release suggested he had been imprisoned in his marriage, which was not at all what he had meant. Marriage had never been to him claustrophobic or limiting – he hated it to be termed so. Marriage had been a great liberating force for him, he had drawn strength from the married state. What he had meant was release not so much in the sense of being freed from bonds but in the sense of absolution. The communicant receiving the sacrament (Robert was not and never had been a communicant) was "released" into Christ, or the church, or something spiritual, some spiritual state that transcended everyday concerns. Robert wanted release in that sort of ill defined way. Everything was too much. He wanted less so that he might grow again. The possibility that he might wither away entirely had not been lost on him. He might return to that unhappy person he had been before he met Anna, forever searching.

He got off the bus and crossed Wandsworth High Street. It was after four o'clock. Betty would be having a fit – he had left no message for her. It was so very unlike him to do this that she would be alarmed and he did not wish to create an atmosphere of alarm in his office. If he was to have no home, his office would be doubly important as a calm place to which he could go, where everything went on absolutely as usual. He wanted to see Betty sitting at her typewriter, solemn and adoring, just as usual. He wanted to hear her little coughs which regularly punctuated the silence, and watch her trot out on errands, her rather small, fat legs hurrying. Betty must know nothing.

Four

Getting home was not something Claire found as arduous as the rest of London's working population, but then she was as fortunate in this aspect of her life as in most others. She lived in New Square, near Lincoln's Inn Fields, a short and interesting walk from her place of employment, in a flat which had been in her family for three generations. Naturally, they were a legal family, the flat being originally the rooms of Claire's great-grandfather, Charles Bayley QC. To keep the family tradition going, Claire's elder brother, Michael, ought to have been residing in the flat and studying at the Bar but Michael had elected to be the manager of a pop group he had formed during his less than satisfactory career at Oundle. So Claire, by default, had the flat and was very pleased with it.

Being pleased did not mean she looked after it. Once, even unto the days of Claire's father, there had been a cleaning lady, a kind of housekeeper, who had looked after all the young gentlemen in residence, but such luxury had disappeared during the 1970s. There was no cleaning lady. Claire was not her own cleaning lady. She had not touched the floors – carpeted in an extremely depressing but very serviceable dark grey Wilton – since she moved in. The mahogany furniture went undusted, the silver unpolished. "Of course," Claire's father and mother had said magnanimously, "you will want to refurbish the place. It is in a bachelor state." They had named a sum she could spend but Claire had not spent it. She was indifferent to her surroundings, lacking as she did any home-making instincts. There was plenty of room for her books, there was a magnificently large desk across which it was a pleasure to spread one's papers, and the bed was wide and comfortable.

Nothing about the flat betrayed the fact that a young lady of twenty-two lived there. There was no underwear draped round the old-fashioned claw-footed green bath, there were no girlish fripperies festooning the large bedroom where the crimson velvet drapes were rarely opened, there were no posters or vases of dried leaves or mementoes of exuberant foreign travels. Letting herself in each evening, Claire felt she hardly disturbed the ghosts who resided there at all. The flat – the rooms – did not belong to her. She had not tried to make them belong. She was merely borrowing them for a season, content to be part of the continuity which existed.

She went to the refrigerator, which held only four pounds of Cox's Orange Pippins, two litres of fresh unsweetened orange juice and some cheddar cheese. She selected an apple, cut a piece of cheese and poured a glass of juice, then went to her desk. It would have been so much better if Anna Osgood had come here – she would have seen at once that there could be no domestic threat from a girl who lived like this. Anna had spoken at length of her home. She had dwelt upon the sunny, shabby rooms and all the significant objects in them and she had said repeatedly that it was more than a building, it was a home. No matter how Claire tried she would be unable to make such a home for Robert. It took years. It did not just happen – it evolved. Without this precious home Robert would be deeply unhappy. Had she thought about this, had it figured in her calculations at all?

That had been before Claire had successfully established that she was not offering Robert a home. There was to be no refuge from his broken marriage, should he break it. Nor was there to be any other marriage, ever. Claire munched her apple, looked out on to the Square, and was glad she had got that in quickly, forcefully. No new marriage. She had said the very thought of marriage was poisonous to her. She had told Robert so. Marriage was a nasty, claustrophobic institution which shut people out from all that was fresh and light and free. And she was not merely quibbling over a word: living together regardless of a marriage ceremony was just as bad.

Anna had been very shocked. In a way, this sort of announcement had clearly helped to deflect the pain that Claire realised Anna was experiencing. Anna had become indignant, then interested in Claire's ideas and had stoutly defended her own. Anna said that far from being a claustrophobic institution marriage was a liberating influence. It was a giver of strength. Sinewy and supple, the muscles of marriage supported every kind of weight that fell upon one in life. Without marriage she, Anna, would be nothing. If it was taken away from her she would be nothing again. It was no good Claire despising her for such an admission; it was true and furthermore it was nothing to be ashamed of. She knew that really – *really* – Robert felt the same. Oh yes, he did. He was merely ill in some way, momentarily un-balanced. Why else did he think he ought to leave his marriage if it was not because Claire wanted to marry him?

Claire realised, apple, cheese and juice finished, that she had not been unaffected by this afternoon's experience. She felt depressed. What depressed her was not just Anna Osgood's attitude, though that was depressing enough, but the thought of all the inescapable complications ahead. She had not, she felt, been unduly naïve about her affair with Robert. Her intelligence had always told her, correctly, that life is never so simple that new human relationships can be made without due heed to those which already existed. One could not go on loving and sleeping with a married man without, in a large measure, taking on his wife and family. They could not just be cut out of one's reckonings like a canker. But she had thought she could at least keep cleanly away from encounters. Robert must cope with those, must go from one to another, comparing and contrasting, laden with guilt. It was no part of her responsibility.

Yet now it was. Anna Osgood's presence had disturbed her, as she had always known it would, though not in the way she had imagined. She had imagined something pathetic. She had seen Anna before, of course, she had even spoken to her, but these public meetings did not count. All they had shown her was a middle-aged, slightly plump, quite plain woman who was badly dressed and conscious of her own ordinariness. It had been an image quite easy to forget. What Claire had feared from a personal confrontation was the realisation that Robert's wife was pitifully weak. She had expected appalling tears, recriminations, bitterness, despair, humiliation. She had expected to be begged to go away. She had thought she would be disgusted. Yet Anna Osgood, though some of her words betrayed all of those feelings, had had about her a certain demonstrable integrity which at the time Claire had found impressive. She had admired Anna for her resolution, her determination that the unacceptable should not be accepted. It was this admiration which was now depressing her.

Claire walked about, her high-heeled shoes making no sound on the thick carpet. Why should she admire Anna? It was not admirable to go behind one's husband's back to see his mistress. It showed an appalling lack of pride. It was not admirable to ask for co-operation in defeating one's husband's expressed wishes. In fact, it was absurd. And yet Claire found it admirable. Robert had always said his wife was the most underestimated woman in the world (his world) and now she saw he was right. She wanted to help preserve the marriage of Robert and Anna Osgood – she, the instrument through which it threatened to split asunder. She damned well would too. But how? Her promise to Anna had been unconditional. It had also been useless.

Robert entered his office almost on tip-toe. What he really wanted to do was get behind his desk – behind those gilt-framed photographs of the family – before Betty looked up. It was a ludicrous notion. His desk was at the far side of the quite large room. Betty's was in the corner, behind the door as one entered, at right angles to his. Robert had never in his life simply stalked past.

In any case, Betty stopped him. She shot upright from her swivel-chair and said,

"Robert!"

"Good heavens – Betty." He knew she was going to ask where on earth he had been, to say she was *very* surprised he had left the office without notice, to bombard him with telephone messages and enquiries from every other person in the building. But he had no lies ready, never would have, he was hopeless.

"Robert, I just discovered – as soon as you'd gone – as soon as I got back from lunch – your letters, yesterday's mail, it got burned accidentally."

"Well, don't worry, Betty."

"I *am* worried. I *have* been worried."

"There was nothing important. I'm sure you've got blacks. Just do them again when you have a minute."

"But there may have been something personal, something I haven't got a black of."

"I don't think so. Don't fret anyway."

She watched him sit down, pick up that manuscript he was to have decided about by noon. He had not even asked how the letters had got burned. All that thought, the sweating over the plausibility of her story – she had even written it out, tying up the loose ends – and he had shown no interest whatsoever. Betty went on typing, watching Robert all the time. There was neither relief nor horror on his face. Nothing had penetrated – he hadn't remembered about Anna's letter and it didn't look as if he was going to. A whole hour went by. It was time for Betty to leave. She stopped typing, put the cover on her typewriter, collected her coat from the stand in the corner.

"Are you going to work late?" she asked.

"What? Oh. Mm. Yes. I am. I was out a long time, wasn't I? Lot to catch up on."

"Shall I ring Anna?"

"Why?"

"If you're going to be late – your supper – it's just considerate, to let her know."

"Oh, she won't mind."

"How do you know?"

"I beg your pardon, Betty?"

"How do you know she won't mind?"

"Well, I've been married to her twenty years. She never has done."

"Good night, then."

Betty paused, torn by the need to make herself as plain as she normally would.

"What is it, Betty?"

"I'm posting those four letters that got burned yesterday. I've re-done them."

"Oh, good."

"But there were five. I had five in my hand. I distinctly remember. Five, Robert. I only typed four but you gave me one you typed or wrote. Definitely. I can't believe you don't recall it."

"Does it matter?"

"Yes! I told you, that letter, the one you wrote, so it must have been important, don't you think, because you hardly ever do your own letters – that letter NEVER GOT POSTED. Whoever it was to never got it. I'm *very* surprised you don't seem to care. Now, goodnight."

Robert stared at Betty's retreating back in amazement. He had never known her bad tempered. Betty Munroe's greatest asset was her phlegmatic nature. She got on with what she had to do and her personality was never intrusive. He wondered if she was worried about something – crossed in love, perhaps – but did Betty have lovers? He didn't think so. She kept herself to herself with his full approval and connivance but he thought she led a remarkably orderly and solitary life. The big excitements in her life were the trips home to Dundee, laden with presents. Her family were all. Occasionally, she spoke about them, about their hard lives, but with a triumphant expression. Perhaps one of them was ill and Betty under strain and he had been brutally preoccupied with his own affairs and not noticed. He resolved to be patient next morning, when Betty would doubtlessly badger him again about the lost letter. He would try very, very hard to remember who he had scribbled some note to. Already, he was rifling through both his In and Out trays and then the drawers of his capacious desk in search of clues as to the nature of this doomed missive. And then of course, quite simply, he remembered.

*　　*　　*

It was not significant, Anna decided, that Robert was not home by six o'clock. He very rarely was. Today he would have returned late to the office from wherever he had been – Betty was embarrassed not to know – and he would stay on to make up for it. He had the habits of a junior clerk and not an executive director. A conscientious junior clerk, that is. He was never good to himself, so far as she was able to see. He did not even claim an office to himself. So Anna left the window and busied herself altering Imogen's skirt. She sat on the golden velvet button-backed armchair near the window and sewed. Downstairs, Harry was watching a noisy television programme and playing snooker at the same time. He hadn't asked where his father was, neither had Imogen. Robert came and went and his presence or other-wise was not often commented on. If he was abroad, the children would be vaguely aware of it but more humble trips were often forgotten about. This sometimes pained him. No exaggerated welcomes or cries of Daddy, you're back, only a few grunts and nods to signify his return was acknowledged. She had always argued this was a sign of their security but Robert could think of quite a few other things it could be a sign of.

The children loved their father. There was no doubt about that, Anna thought, as she bit a length off a piece of cotton. But she had to admit that he was not as important in their lives as she was. When they were little there were faces pressed to the window for her return if she so much as went shopping for the day and left them with Robert, even though he played wonderful games with them, was much more fun than she was. Now that they were older, teenagers, they tended to argue with him a great deal. They wouldn't listen to his advice, nor let him voice opinions they thought dull. Only Imogen had any real contact with him.

Anna trembled as she rethreaded her needle. It was quite

unthinkable that Robert should risk hurting his younger daughter, who had been hurt so badly already at such a tender age. Imogen was afraid of life. Now, wherever she went, whatever she did there was this "but-what-if—" approach to everything. She could hardly cross a road alone ("but what if a car goes too fast and. . ."), nor walk along a pavement without hugging the hedge or wall and even then, "but what if a car mounts the pavement and . . ." To get her into a car was virtually impossible. They had given up trying. When they went to the country she had to be sedated and Anna sat in the back cradling her in her arms for extra security. Everywhere she saw lightning streaking out of a blue, blue sky to strike her down. She still had nightmares, which extended to daymares. The low sobbing in the early hours of the morning would produce a chalk-white face at breakfast and often repeated vomiting until it was time to sleep again. Sammy, Imogen's friend who had died in the crash, appeared often to haunt her. There was death and loss in front of the girl's eyes at every turn. Imogen ought to be a trump card in the game she was playing.

The temptation was very real. At seven (but Robert had been later, often, hope need not be abandoned) Anna got up and went in search of Imogen. She was not in the living room with Harry, nor in the kitchen. Anna climbed the stairs to her bedroom, a little fearfully, wanting to find Imogen happily listening to records but knowing she was more likely to find her unhappily crouched on the bed in a silent room with every lamp blazing. She knocked. Imogen said come in. Relief made Anna smile over-enthusiastically.

"How nice," she said, and picked up a magazine out of which Imogen had cut a picture to stick on the old screen her grandmother had given her. "I've got a big bundle down-stairs – of magazines. I'll bring them up. I wish Harry would do something constructive like this."

The scissors fell from Imogen's hand.

"It's boring really. Is Dad home?"

Anna's heart leapt.

"No. No, he isn't. Not yet. I was just thinking of ringing him, as a matter of fact. To see if he's going to be much later. Would you do it for me while I . . . see to the oven?"

"If you like."

"You could do it from his study."

"Shall I say you're waiting?"

"No. Oh no – I'm not really. I just . . . wondered. About a meal. You could just say I wondered."

She went downstairs quickly, but paused on the half-landing, listening to Imogen's light step on the stairs, the study door opening, the telephone lifting, the dialling, the silence, the pause, the repeated dialling.

"There's no reply," Imogen called.

"Oh well, not to worry," she called back. "I expect he's on his way."

They met in the foyer of the National Theatre, Robert and Claire. A favourite meeting place for them. Robert took Anna often to the National Theatre and was always dropping in to collect tickets – it was a natural place to meet, to be perhaps seen. Robert took his car to a street near Claire's flat, then got a taxi across the river.

"You look no better," Claire said. "Did you sleep, last night?"

"No."

"Silly man."

"I thought it would be wrong to come to you."

"Right, wrong, wrong, right. You should listen to yourself sometime, Robert. Really."

"I didn't sleep at all and I've had the most terrible day. I can't bear it."

"What?"

"Everything. You're so cool. You're even amused, aren't you? Aren't you? You're almost laughing. You can't believe the torment I'm experiencing."

"Oh, Robert. Don't dramatise a perfectly ordinary occurrence."

"What am I to do then?"

"Either do something positive or shut up."

"I went home today. At lunch-time. I just got this overwhelming impulse to go home. I thought it would help me, to be there, in the middle of the afternoon when it was empty."

"And did it?"

"It wasn't empty. Sarah was there, home from school early. I could see Anna hadn't told her about the letter."

"Good."

"It worries me, though. She's so brave, Anna. I'm afraid for her."

Claire was about to ask if he was sure Anna had got his wretched letter, which would have ruined everything, when Robert blurted out, "Actually, I'm worried she didn't even get the letter."

"Well, you'll have to ask her, won't you?"

"I can't. How can I? But Betty says my letters didn't get posted yesterday. They got burned or something."

"How extraordinary. How?"

"Oh, I don't know. I didn't ask – what does it matter? – the point is Betty says they definitely were not posted."

Anna had not mentioned her trip to Betty but Claire saw at once her stratagem and admired her all over again.

"Well then, Robert, you're reprieved. Congratulations."

"Don't be fatuous."

"I'm not. You *are* reprieved. The situation is as before. All day you've made yourself ill with remorse and terror over what you've done and now you find you haven't, after all, done it. You should be delighted."

"Well, I'm not."

"Just go home to your loving wife with nothing to forgive and every time you get this stupid urge to write absurd confessional letters just remember today – circle it on your calendar – the point of no return from which you have successfully returned."

Robert bent his head. People all around were going into the different auditoriums as the bell went. Soon he and Claire would have to go. He knew he ought to tell her about telling Sarah what he had done – was doing – but he was afraid of Claire's contempt. Or even worse, loud laughter. So he kept quiet, taking in the implications of Anna, his wife, perhaps after all not knowing of his infidelity but Sarah, his daughter, being well informed. Nothing had been resolved. He had only introduced another complication.

It would be very nice to go home, now, to Anna. But could he look her in the eyes, hold her? His head ached with trying to remember where he had said he was going last night. Anywhere would do – it didn't really matter. He quite often returned from business trips too bored and tired to want to talk about it. Anna would understand, no doubt about it. He only had to sigh and pass a weary hand over his eyes, both quite easy to do, and all would be well. He could leave Sarah a note – oh God no, no more notes. He would catch her in the morning, give her a lift to school. It would be embarrassing, and then of course there was the future. Sarah would always *know*. Would it matter? That depended on what he was going to do.

"It depends what I'm going to do," he found himself saying aloud.

"I think," Claire said, very clearly, "we should get one thing clear after all this. *You* do what you want to do or need to do or feel you have to do, but I, I do nothing. I refuse to say I will give you up. I refuse to say I cannot give you up. You may not be a free agent as far as poor Anna is concerned but you are as far as I am concerned."

"You always say 'poor' Anna. I wish you wouldn't. It's so condescending. She isn't poor. I don't want you pitying her."

"Why should I do that?"

"Then why say 'poor'?"

"It was a term of endearment, thoughtlessly chosen."

"You can't want to love her."

"No, I don't. But I find myself unable to help it."

"You don't even know her."

"As you keep pointing out. Look, Robert, you wrestling with your conscience is not an edifying sight. Let's go."

"All right. But it's late."

"You won't be much after eight – Anna will think nothing of it."

They walked along the embankment, through Middle Temple Lane, across the Strand and so to New Square. Neither of them talked. Robert had his arm round Claire's waist and she had hers round his. They were well matched in height and walked in perfect harmony. Robert kept thinking that there could be nothing wrong in what felt so right. There were never any scenes with Claire, no ugly recriminations. She seemed content with so little. It was he who was discontented with his superabundance of affections. He breathed deeply and ordered himself to live in the present. Now, here, the lights of the boats on the river winking away in the shiny blackness. Now, here, passing the gaunt and grey bulk of the Temple. Now, entering Claire's flat; now, watching her undress; now, in bed and loving her. He tried to shut out of the perimeters of his inner eye disturbing images from the past and the future – faces, scenes, buildings.

He tried to turn off the relentless sound of his own voice arguing with him. If he could let go, drift, not seek to command the action, what might not be achieved?

He slept. Claire did not. She got up after a while, covering Robert with a blanket, and went softly into the bathroom, where she ran a bath and lay in soapsuds, hiding. She was beginning to feel sorry for Robert. He could not help what had happened. He was an innocent abroad and she, so much younger, was cunning and knowing. She resented the way in which she found herself thinking she ought to have kept away from him, for his own good. *She* had known, from that first meeting, what would happen, with a little help, her help. He had not. She had had no patience with the view that marriages should not be wilfully broken. She had no intention of breaking Robert's marriage and if an affair – a relationship – with her broke it, it was not worth much anyway. If not her, someone else. But now, six months later, she saw the flaws in her thinking. Robert was too good. He did not want it both ways, as most men did. Love-making, talking, being together – these were not simply pleasant diversions for him: he gave himself. She saw how he was trapped, loving Anna, loving her. She ought to make it easy for him, and go, remove herself from his life entirely. But as she had explained to Anna, today, that would be no good to Robert. He had to work things out for himself.

But what a mess he was making of it. When she went back into the bedroom, Robert was still asleep and it was nearly eight o'clock. Anna would be beginning to despair. Something drastic would have to be done.

Tom left about eleven o'clock, perfectly amicably. Usually he resented Sarah's insistence that he should leave before whoever she was babysitting for came home, but tonight he was a good boy, he went without fuss. Sarah found Tom's constant desire for confrontation with authority of every kind tiring and childish. There was really no need to slap people in the face. She herself avoided it at all costs, realising with a rare maturity that it was quite possible to do what one wished without pointing this out.

But tonight Tom had been obedient. He had responded with a degree of sensitivity to her anxiety about Robert and Anna which had surprised her. She had hopes of him, of their relationship turning into something more than a sexual coupling. The truth was, there was not much chance for Tom unless it did – he was quite frankly not much good at sex, in Sarah's opinion. She had yet to meet any boy who was. All of them were far too eager, far too over-excited, it was all over much too quickly, leaving her thinking, "so what". She had scaled no orgasmic heights, only glimpsed them tantalisingly in the distance. Her sense of frustration was high. Though she had no worries about being frigid – her physical state of readiness was unmistakable – she fretted over her ability to select a suitable mate.

She knew of course that her mother, that Anna, would say sex without love could never be any good. They did not discuss it these days, when it was highly relevant, but Sarah could remember far-off juvenile days when the subject had been given frequent experimental airings. Some level of emotional commitment was necessary before love-making could be a wonderful experience, Anna had said. A lover had to be a friend, the place and time had to be right. Otherwise, it was squalid. Sarah could not remember how Anna had come to impart this knowledge, nor how old she had been when she had heard it (with total disinterest), but she had a clear recollection of automatically and instinctively rejecting it. Not that she had said so, either then or since. She had just known it would be pointless ever discussing sex with Anna.

Yet she did not want Anna to get her come-uppance. The

thought of her hearing about Robert's mistress caused Sarah inexpressible pain. The pity of it hurt. She was glad she had not been in the house when that stupid letter was read. Surely Anna must have cried out? Surely, wherever she was in the house, she would have heard it? The same sort of cry, Sarah imagined, as Anna gave when the policeman came to the door and said Imogen was injured. Really, one only ran from that kind of anguish. There were no defences possible. She could not see, whichever way she looked, how Anna could withstand this violent rending asunder of all she held so precious and thought so perfect.

Tom had, in the end, stopped sneering. For the first time he had spoken of what it had really meant to him when his father left home. He said how he had always worshipped him, though seeing at the same time that he was unworthy of worship. He had often sat, like a dog, outside his father's room, just waiting for him to get up and come out and pay him attention. Then there had been his mother's distress, the anger and jealousy fusing into irrational violence – things thrown, things (unspeakable still) said. And finally the shame of her lover, young and callow, for whom she bought kites and roller-skates, upon whose twenty-year-old body she fawned. It made you sick, Tom said. They hadn't deserved children, that was his opinion. All that slob about love and marriage: they would have been better off as alley cats.

Sarah had begun to like him all over again. She had enjoyed lying quietly talking with him more than she ever had fucking. If they had had more time she was sure their love-making would have been successful that night. At the back of her mind were the beginnings of the idea that poor Anna might just be right. Not that now it would be any comfort to her. Nothing would. Sarah badly wanted to take home comfort with her when she went but could think of none. Should she say she knew or pretend otherwise? Would

Anna be helped more by sympathy or ignorance of her plight? She had shown she just wanted to carry on as normal and Sarah felt she must follow that lead.

Gillian and husband came home at midnight, fat and smug, boringly full of their meal and the awful film they had seen. Sarah could not wait to get out, but the rites of babysitting had to be observed, the money solemnly calculated and counted out, the thanks (totally insincere) expressed on both sides. Sarah was so relieved to get out, to walk the short distance home and open the door on her own home where the atmosphere was freer.

She let herself in as quietly as possible and locked the door. Taking her shoes off she crept up the stairs. On the second landing she found herself incapable of passing her parents' bedroom for thinking of Anna lying there, alone and grieving. Would she be asleep? Hesitant, Sarah stood there. Tears were in her eyes. Slowly, she peered round the open door, resolved to act if Anna spoke. But she did not speak. She appeared to be sound asleep and beside her, on the same pillow, was Robert's head.

Five

"What's going on?" Harry said, in amazement. They were all down for breakfast, all sitting round the table at eight o'clock, with places properly set.

It was always sunny in the morning in the kitchen, should there be any sun. A dangerous illusion of real heat was always created. The rest of the day the sun did not come into the kitchen which was, being east-facing, cold. To counter this the central heating radiator was large, running a full twelve feet along the outer wall, and, therefore, for that one hour of morning sunshine, the room was often excessively hot. They were all always reluctant to leave it.

But they were also all fairly reluctant to enter it at all. Not even Anna's highly developed sense of family spirit required her to have an organised breakfast for everyone. She had given up trying long ago. They all left at different times, they all had different breakfast requirements: she was content to leave well alone. So in dribs and drabs they came, fixing their own breakfasts, Harry always last and greediest and in a rush. His bad temper fairly burst upon them.

"I don't want an egg," he said, as though offered poison. "I'll get what I want *myself*. I hate people in the kitchen in the morning."

Nobody spoke. Nobody knew why they were there anyway – it had been an accident, surely. Anna was there (fully dressed) because she had been up since half past six, full of joy and health, so grateful and emotional that it was too dangerous to stay inside. She had been out for a walk with the dog, all the way to the woods, where she had cried and smiled in privacy and returned home chastened and humble. Sarah was there because she thought she ought to be. Solidarity was surely required. It had been the most awful effort but she had gone to sleep determined to do it and had got up the moment she wakened for fear of her resolution wavering. She was now rather cross, seeing her magnanimous gesture as rather unnecessary after all. Imogen was there because, as usual, she was afraid. A by now over-familiar feeling of apprehension had come upon her last night and had gone on building up ever since. Something was going to happen, something awful, something she could not prevent. Not even the sun and her family around her in the kitchen could completely allay her fears.

And Robert was there because he was in a state of delayed shock and did not know what he was doing. He had got up the minute Anna woke him by leaving the bed. He had stumbled into the bathroom, showered, dressed (very formally) and he had been downstairs sitting at the head of the table like a dummy, reading *The Times*, ever since. He hardly dared to look over the top of the paper, but when he did he saw his family around him as though waiting for an announcement. When Harry – crashing the grill in and out – said rudely, "Where've you been lately anyway?" he was electrified. They all seemed to turn slowly, expectantly, towards him. "Oh," he said, "nowhere much. On business. Leeds."

"I heard you come back," Imogen said, and blushed. It implied she had been waiting nervously, or so she felt. She had.

That was all. Everyone went on with crunching toast, sipping coffee. Soon Harry had gone, leaving a sound trail of slammed doors. The doorbell went. It was Imogen's two friends, come to collect her (as they had done since the accident) to take her to school. Her hatred of both of them, for their kindness, was just beginning to show itself. "Oh hell," she said. Anna went to the door with her, for support, leaving Robert and Sarah momentarily alone.

"Well?" Sarah leaned over and whispered. Robert frowned, shook his head.

"Do you want a lift to school?" he said, aloud.

"What time are you going?"

"Now. I've got a lot to do. The traffic will be terrible but I'll have to try."

"Right. Yes. I'll just get my stuff." And as Anna came back and began clearing up, "Dad's giving me a lift."

"Already? You don't usually go so early, Robert. Is it wise?"

She looked at him in concern. He searched the look: concern for what? Anything deeper than traffic problems? Last night, when he returned, there had been the same concern – for his tiredness, his journey, his hunger. There had been an affectionate kiss and comfort. But perhaps, pushed out of her car by Claire in a somnolent state, he had not been alert enough to recognise anything else. Now, already, the normal tempo of his marriage beat strongly away and he could no longer discern irregularities. If any were present, if Anna was dissembling, he could not tell.

"Will you be home early? Will we leave early and have supper at the cottage? It's going to be a beautiful weekend – shall we leave early?"

"Yes," he said, because he wanted to make one firm decision, a decision he felt would put him back on the tracks firmly. He did not want to have to think about the weekend as being anything but the expected one. And on a beautiful Friday morning he always would have said yes, eagerly, to the suggestion of getting away to the country early. After he had said it, he took a deep breath and went over to Anna and put one hand on each of her shoulders and looked into her surprised eyes. "Right," he said, "I will be home early. Sorry about . . ."

"You couldn't help it," she said. "Trains and things."

"Quite. Anyway. I'll be home early."

"Shall we have spare ribs?"

"Mm. Yes. Lovely."

"And do you want to take your electric saw – for that tree – you said next time it ought to come down, before the winter?"

"Yes."

"I've got the bulbs. I'll do those. Should I *make* Harry come?"

"Definitely."

"He'll swear. He does so hate it now. But this might be the last weekend for ages, the end of the year and all that, though I like winter in the country . . ."

"Ready, Dad?"

"Will you come, Sarah?" Anna called. "To the cottage, a last weekend, just for once?"

"Oh, all right. As it's the last weekend. Dad, come on."

Elizabeth, about to put a note through Lucy's door to say she could not after all make coffee next week, was caught in the act and dragged in. She always lost when eye to eye with Lucy, or even voice to voice. Lucy could not be denied. No good saying, "I really must dash," in reply to Lucy's, "Come in a minute," because Lucy ignored it. The battle commenced – there was just no way in which it could be shortened. A dozen variations on No, I cannot, will not, must not, met by increasingly loud assurances that she could, would, had to. In the end, unless she literally had the car engine running and a convincing appointment to flourish, it seemed to require too much energy to refuse. If Lucy cared so much, if it was so important to her, then she must be given in to.

Anna Osgood was in the kitchen, radiant. It was the only word Elizabeth could think of which would adequately describe Anna's state of well-being. She looked so young, so fresh, so full of health and happiness. There was about her a glow of vitality which lit Lucy's slummy, untidy, colourful kitchen. "Hello, Elizabeth," Anna said, with such immense kindness and warmth that Elizabeth immediately remembered what Lucy had said about Anna running her down. "Hello," she replied, hurriedly, stiff and obviously ill at ease. She didn't want to add, "I haven't seen you for ages," in case this implied a rebuke.

"I haven't seen you for ages," Anna said. "My fault – always rushing. I'm rushing this morning really but Lucy was persuasive." She winked at Elizabeth, who smiled rather primly. "She said I looked as if I needed some coffee."

"You're always rushing, both of you," Lucy said, clattering about in her usual disorganised way, making it seem as if she was making a seven-course meal instead of a cup of coffee. "I don't know why you do it, why you can't just relax and take life as it comes like I do?" Anna and Elizabeth exchanged amused smiles behind her back. She looked like Alice in Wonderland, that long blonde hair streaming down her flowered overall. Until she turned round.

"As you both *say* you're rushing it didn't seem worth making proper coffee."

"I'm not just saying it," Anna protested. "We're going to the country this evening. I have to shop and cook and have everything ready to load into the car the minute Robert arrives home."

"You've been doing it for years," Lucy said. "You can do it standing on your head."

"You have been doing it for years, haven't you?" Elizabeth said. "I remember seeing you when we first moved in, ten years ago – no, twelve – all those small children and all that stuff you had to take. I remember thinking how nice it looked but half wondering how on earth it could be worth all the chaos, even though you made it look easy."

"I've never known how it could be worth it," Lucy said. "I don't believe it is, either."

"Peter and I tried it," Elizabeth said, "that cottage we had near Diss, did either of you ever see it? But it didn't work out. It was beautiful, I loved it, but somehow the driving – we used to fight so much over whether to go – then somehow it was exhausting, a strain. It didn't work." Her voice trailed off.

"Robert and Anna don't fight," Lucy said, loudly. "Any normal couple would but they don't." It was meant to be affectionate but did not sound it. "Oh, we have our differences," Anna said.

"That's the first time you've admitted that. It'll be divorce next." Elizabeth flushed, a deep, dark, mottled red. "Oh Elizabeth – I'm sorry – it was a joke, I mean a joke about Anna and Robert – I didn't think."

"No reason why you should. It isn't an illness you know, Lucy. I don't expect people to handle me carefully. I just find it difficult to be philosophical about. I do still hate being divorced."

"Of course you do." Lucy said, soothingly.

"I couldn't bear it," Anna said, abruptly. "I would probably have a nervous breakdown."

"That's not what you said a few months ago."

"I've thought about it since then. It's more complicated than I imagined – I mean, once I thought really deeply about it."

"What made you do that?" There was gleam in Lucy's ever-watchful, hopeful eye.

"It was – a friend of mine, nobody you know, happily married twenty years and suddenly her husband is having an affair with a young girl."

"Oh, it's always young girls," Lucy interrupted, "always sex."

"No, it isn't quite that, in this case. My friend says their sex-life is very happy . . ."

"They all say that. Pride."

"Well, I believe her, actually. And the thing is, her husband still loves her."

"That's another thing they all say."

"He says he does. And the girl in the case doesn't want to marry him either."

"Crazy."

"She just wants things to go on. She doesn't see why not. But my friend does."

"Of course she does. What's she going to do?"

It was, Elizabeth supposed, the reason why any of them liked Lucy at all. No matter how remote the people – people she neither knew nor would ever know – Lucy was always interested in human sagas. She could become so easily fascinated by dramatic tales of a friend of a friend of a friend that she was quite capable of retelling them with tremendous gusto and even less sense of involvement to an even wider audience. And afterwards, perhaps weeks afterwards, she would show she had not forgotten. "You know that friend of your friends," she would say, "the one whose husband was having the affair with the daughter of the man who . . . how is she?" It was a breathless hunger for contact with drama but it was also kindness.

So now Lucy bent forward eagerly, ready to cross-examine Anna, and Elizabeth felt she could not stand it another minute. The two of them could go on quite happily all morning without her. But to her surprise, when she stood up and picked up her bag, Anna got up too. "No, Lucy, I absolutely must go. Thank you for the coffee. Have a good weekend." Lucy said if they hung on a moment she would come with them but they all heard the baby wake up screaming and not even Lucy could carry the pretence off. She watched them depart wistfully. There was nothing Lucy liked better than sweeping down to the shops, three abreast, laughing and chattering.

Actually they walked in silence. Anna was sweating at her near escape. It was not that she needed to be told that discussing one's private affairs (even when they were not affairs) with Lucy was absolutely fatal but what she had not realised was how strong the need to confide in someone would be. She had longed to test out her own story and had almost succumbed to Lucy's interest. How unbelievably lucky that Elizabeth -- silent, disapproving -- had inhibited her sufficiently barely to begin the saga. Elizabeth had protected her.

At the corner, they paused. Elizabeth was going to work, Anna to the shops.

"I wish," Anna said, "you would come and see me sometime."

"I will. Thank you."

"Why don't we fix a date?"

"Well, I'm a bit busy at the moment. There seem to be a

lot of extra things to do. Let's leave it for a bit, shall we, till I get sorted out? I'm not quite sure what I'm going to do. I might move – sell the house."

"Must you? Wouldn't it be an upheaval, I mean for the children, when, I mean, with –?"

"The children don't care what happens. That's the plain truth. And anyway I'm sick of making decisions for the children's sake. I need to make some for my own sake. I only seem to have had rights when I was married. Now nobody seems to think I have any."

"It isn't that at all. I only meant –"

"Oh, I know what you meant. Lucy told me you think I have no spirit –"

"How *wicked* of her!"

"It doesn't matter. You know what she's like. She can't help it, gossip is a disease with her and she's never known the rules, she doesn't even know there are rules. I didn't hold it against you. But it isn't that I don't care about Peter – I do – and about our marriage, it's that I literally have no energy. None. I'm deflated. I can't stop being sensible and practical after a lifetime of being like that. I don't approve of my own behaviour but I can't change it. And of course I keep seeing Peter's point of view, that's the most demoralising thing of all. I'm just so bloody understanding."

"Elizabeth –"

"No, don't say a word. I shouldn't have started. I just don't want you to despise me, that's all."

"I *don't* despise you."

"You do."

"Elizabeth! I –"

Anna was just about to cry that she knew exactly how she felt because she had just had an enormous shock herself, that yesterday – and Gillian stopped alongside in her car. "Mothers' Meeting?" she said cheerfully. "Can I give anyone a lift? I'm going to the shops." Elizabeth said goodbye. Anna got numbly into the car. "Whatever were you talking about?" Gillian said. "You looked so upset."

Betty could hardly wait to get into the office. She cut down considerably on her morning rituals in order to be in early and she did not attempt to wait for a bus. Living in Clapham as she did – in a small flat which faced on to the Common – it was exactly half an hour's walk. If she got a bus it was ten minutes, but the buses were irregular and the time they took variable. Whenever Betty particularly wanted to be on time she walked.

This morning her instincts told her Robert would be early, to catch up on yesterday's lapse from grace. If he did not look any better and if he still did not seem to have remembered the lost letter of such momentous significance then she was going to ring Anna. All night her head had seethed with questions and she had worked herself into quite a rage over how she had been used. Yes, Anna had *used* her, without doing her the compliment of trusting her. That was not good enough.

All her life Betty had been "used". She had been used shamelessly by her family, who were not even really her family anyway. She had been an orphan, then a foster-child, taken in with two others to eke out the family income, and kept on because she was good and obedient and very, very useful. The home she got in return was clean and safe and not without warmth and occasional affection. "Betty is the best of the lot of you," was a roar used against the natural children but it was always followed by, "I bless the day I took the puir wee thing in," which Betty hated. She had not been "taken in". She had been applied for. There were official forms. There were visits. Money changed hands regularly. There was, thankfully, little charity involved.

Because of this Betty worked if anything harder. She was a willing maid-of-all-work after school and once she was working she gave over half her wage to her foster-mother, who was secretly appalled, even made nervous, by such munificence. When Betty announced she was going to London it was worse than the roof falling in and her assurance that she would continue to pay her dues not believed.

Of course, she paid this imaginary conscience money. Never once did her foster-mother demur. None of her own children gave her a penny but Betty's £10 a week was pocketed and hardly remarked on. It meant enormous self-sacrifice for Betty but she went on making it grimly. If they were not going to say it was too much, that they no longer really needed it, it was too good of her, they were ashamed to take it – then she was going to go on sending it.

Betty had been used by men, and women too. She was so sturdily independent that all her life people had used her. She got stood up on dates, let down by friends and never complained. She was obliging, loyal and expected to take knocks. Twice she had been in love, twice the lover deserted her and she never sought to know why. This was not because she was feeble: on the contrary, only a fighter with a high degree of self-respect could have made anything of the sort of start in life Betty Munroe had had. But her courage and strength she kept inside herself, preferring that the world should see her as stony-faced in adversity. She knew when she was being used and that was enough. She had come to suspect, in her thirtieth year, that everyone permanently exploited everyone else.

Except, of course, Robert Osgood. Robert did not use Betty. He was quite unlike the average boss. He treated her at all times with courtesy and made sure she was neither overworked nor underpaid. She served no confessional purpose, was not either a drudge or a sounding-board. And so she had grown bold, nurtured in such an atmosphere. She had begun to expect explanations and almost to demand consultation in matters by which she was affected. The silent acceptance of her lot had stopped. Now, with Anna's request, she saw it all beginning again. She was furious with herself – her old self – for being taken advantage of. Anna Osgood had assumed, rightly, that she could be told to do anything at the merest hint that it was for the sake of Robert's happiness. Anyone with a grain of self-respect would have asked for more information, would not have allowed themselves to be bamboozled as she had done. And what had Anna thought of her for so meekly accepting her instructions? Very little. There was no reward gained in this life by compliance. Furthermore, she might, through the best of intentions, have done a dangerous thing. How could she know that when Anna said it was for Robert's own good this was true? Wasn't Robert the best judge of that?

She came into the office, first into the building, quite clear in her own mind. She would ring Anna Osgood even before Robert did or did not arrive. She would ask for more information, straight out, just like that. The thought of another day full of worry (possibly unjustified) was insupportable.

But Robert came in just as she was taking her coat off. "Morning, Betty," he said with his usual beautiful smile. "I'm in bright and early to make up for yesterday. Sorry about yesterday. I wasn't myself – tell you about it sometime. Now, let's get down to it, shall we?"

"Yes," Betty said.

Sarah found it almost impossible to concentrate at school. She wished for the old, regimented pre-sixth-form days when she had not had to programme herself but could sit at the back of the class and daydream the hours away without anyone noticing. But her tutor group for English was small and there was no escape from the complexities of *Paradise Lost*, Book Nine. Her head ached with the shutting out of larger problems than Milton could ever have known.

If yesterday her father had been distraught and in pieces, today he had annoyed her even more by being enigmatic.

"Well?" she had asked, as soon as they were in the car together.

"I came home," he said. He swung the car round crazily. She wished he were a slower driver, less confident, more careful.

"I can see that. But have you – you know – I mean, what did Mum say?"

"She was asleep."

"Dad!"

"No, she was. Almost, anyway. She very quickly went to sleep after I got home."

"You mean nothing was said?"

"No."

"And you didn't say anything either?"

"No."

"But – did she cry? Or what?"

"No, she didn't cry. She just asked me if I was tired and said poor me. Then we went to sleep."

Aware that they were near the corner of the school, Sarah said quickly, "So what happens now?"

"I'd like you just to forget it, Sarah. I shouldn't have said what I said anyway." He turned and smiled at her, weakly, looking for complicity. She turned away and got out into the cold.

It just wasn't even half clear whether he had chucked this Claire or not, whether her mother had forgiven him, whether everything would now go on as before. He was so stupid, she was so silly. God knew what a hash might still be made. Neither of them seemed capable of talking to the other and yet when had they ever done anything else? The hours and hours she had heard them talking to each other about bugger all and now it was trusting silences.

Her mother had been so happy this morning. It was obscene. All tremulous and adoring like a young bride, all grateful, as though she had been delivered from evil. And her father had been so false, so prim and straight-backed and *bland*. Neither of them seemed to appreciate that the ice below was still very thin. Sarah saw exactly what would happen: Robert would keep away from this Claire for a while and then he would succumb to her charms and then the whole scenario would be repeated, this time with disastrous consequences. Nothing had been faced up to. Anna, her mother, was going to keep her fingers crossed and not do a bloody thing – she would *never* have it out with Robert. All she wanted was to keep him at any cost. Neither of them had the slightest idea how to behave.

Sarah saw how, if they had not been married, twenty years would have vanished in a day. They were supported, both of them, by this amorphous thing called marriage. Not the ceremony, not the piece of paper, but the emotional edifice. It was something not easily destroyed, not without a great deal of strength and violence. The underpinnings were sound, the construction good. Neither of them could just jump out of the window. She wondered if this Claire understood that, or if she should be told.

"Don't think," Claire had whispered in his ear before she pushed him into the car. "Don't think, Robert. Don't think." The gentle instruction had followed him into the house, into Anna's arms, and he had obeyed it. Still dreamy with remembered sleep, he had had no difficulty in preserving

85

his somnolent state. Not to think was desirable. The sheets were different, cooler and heavier, and the faint scent of washed hair, washed in something lemony, had not been there and neither had the pillow, which he had missed. The light was different, grey and creamy, not a chink before, and the arms were softer, fuller, the body more comfortable, less exciting. So he had not thought, just let events take their course, and they had, and he was no less satisfied and happy than he had been.

Now, in daytime, in office time, that quality of calm had not quite left him. Though he was making rapid decisions, though Betty was taking his confident dictation as fast as she could go (which was very fast), he was still not thinking with one half of his brain. It was not like yesterday, he was not disintegrating nor in a mental panic, but he was still far away from himself. Little by little he lifted a blind in his head and peeped at the state of his thoughts – quick, furtive, sneaky looks at the state of play. All they revealed to him was that, miraculously, the worst had not apparently happened. Everything was as it had been. But no, Sarah knew, unless he had convinced her she had not known, and that he doubted. But the point was, Anna did not know. It was like the day before the bomb fell. He didn't have to drop it again. The face of the earth had not been destroyed, there was no need to take to shelters.

Then Betty said, at the end of their long session, when they paused for coffee, "Robert. I would like to talk to you."

"Yes?" he said, quite unsuspecting.

"Yesterday I told you a lie."

"Really, Betty?" He smiled. Betty's puritanism was often a source of amusement to them all. Sometimes it became so extreme it was a nuisance.

"I said some of your letters didn't get posted."

"That's right. It doesn't matter. I was quite glad, really, that they didn't."

For a fraction of a second Betty frowned and hesitated but then she pressed on. "They did," she said.

"Oh."

"I did post them. How *could* they have got burned? I mean, we haven't an incinerator, have we?"

"Haven't we?"

"Of course we haven't, Robert. Nor a fire. How *could* they have got burned? If only you had asked me *how* they got burned, but you didn't."

"I didn't think."

"Exactly. Anyway, they did not get burned. They got posted, all of them."

"Oh."

"Did you remember which one you wrote yourself?"

"Yes. I wrote to Anna – to my wife."

"Ah," Betty said, a long-drawn-out, relaxing noise. "Well, there you are. It *was* posted." Robert looked suitably bewildered. "So you see, nobody could have stopped it." There was a long pause. Robert looked stunned. If only he would ask her why she had said she had burned the letter without her having to force the information upon him. "I'm very sorry I lied to you. I've never done it before and I won't ever do it again."

"Why did you lie, Betty?"

The relief made her slightly incoherent, her Scottish accent thicker. "Anna asked me to. When I went out to lunch yesterday there she was, waiting, and she took me to lunch and said she'd had this letter which she wanted you to think hadn't been sent and would I pretend I hadn't sent it and that it was for your good. I wouldn't have done it if she hadn't said that. For the sake of your happiness, she said."

"Good God."

"I agreed. I don't know why, but I did. She's your wife, she seemed so sure she knew best, and I believed her. Then you seemed so ill and miserable – it seemed to fit in – so I pretended and all night I've regretted it. I shouldn't have done it without knowing *why*. I'm dumb. I just follow instructions."

"You're not dumb, Betty, not in the least."

To his consternation Robert saw she was crying. Her head was lowered almost to her tweed-skirt-covered knees and her tightly drawn back brown hair, ferociously pinned back behind her ears, could not conceal the tears. She was the first to cry. He had not cried; Anna, to his knowledge, had not cried; Claire had not cried and Sarah most certainly had not cried. The pathos had got to Betty first, poor idealistic vulnerable Betty.

"Betty dear, don't cry," he said, going over to her. "It really doesn't matter. It doesn't make any difference." But even as he patted her awkwardly he saw that it did. His blissful not-thinking stage passed. His head throbbed. He was back in yesterday's hell. "Betty," he said, "I think I'd better tell you all about it. Take the telephone off the hook and make some more coffee."

Claire did not expect to hear from Robert until after the weekend. She did not want to. This time it was she who wanted a very big breathing space indeed. She rang her mother and said she was coming down (to Rye, where the family home was) for the weekend. Her mother asked if she was bringing a nice young man and though she had said it teasingly her voice said never mind in a sad way.

Claire had no doubt at all that this would only be a hiatus in their affair. After all, she had not promised Anna to withdraw. She had made it plain that this might seem the obvious thing to do but she would not do it. All she had guaranteed was that Robert would return to Anna that night. But she would not shut either her door or her heart to him. If Anna thought she could totally reclaim her husband then she could try. If she thought pretending he had never written that confessional letter would do it then that was fine. If, in general, hiding her head in the sand was what she wanted to do then she, Claire, would aid and abet her: up to a point. She would help the marriage go on, if it could be helped. But what made Claire unhappy as she threw a few things in a bag was the beginnings of a new fear in herself. Something was changing, a new attitude was crystallising. It scared her. Before Robert wrote his beastly letter which Anna refused to receive, before Anna came to seek her help, she had felt quite free. Now the dark edges of doubt crept into her mind. She hardly dared to admit it to herself but there was a new reluctance to be so obliging. Everyone was assuming that she had no feelings herself. She knew she had encouraged this belief, but it did not matter: it should not be assumed that because she did not want to break Robert's precious marriage she was therefore prepared to give him up. She had not made this plain to Anna, out of cowardice. She must do so. Anna and Robert would have to adapt to the modern notion of what marriage could accommodate.

And this was what frightened her.

Six

Betty stared at Robert, unbelievably distressed. She simply could not believe her ears. Robert had changed before her very eyes. He no longer seemed that wonderfully reassuring word, so hated by the English teacher at school, "nice". His niceness had evaporated, leaving him as doubtful as all the other people in her life.

"Well," she said, when she saw he had finished and was waiting for her to comment, waiting trustingly. "I'm not going to say I quite understand. I think it's terrible, awful. How *could* you? How could you let a cheap affair with a girl like that spoil your marriage? I think it's disgusting. I think you ought to be ashamed of yourself."

"I am."

"It doesn't do any good though, does it, just saying 'I am' like that? I'm surprised, very surprised, at you."

"I knew you would be."

"I'd rather not have known. I don't want to be involved in

all this deceit. I'm just your secretary."

"And friend."

"I don't know about that. It isn't true, is it? I'm not really your friend. Only in the office."

"You're still a friend."

"I don't think I want to be, now."

"Oh Betty – I mean, I know you despise me now but it shouldn't really make any difference to *us*, should it?"

"It does."

"But why should it? My morals are my own business – my personal life, that is."

"You've just made them mine, by telling me."

"No, I haven't. I only told you to clear things up."

"Well, it hasn't. Things aren't cleared up. They're messier than ever."

There was a long silence, but Betty did not move. Robert regarded her closely. Her cheeks – lovely fat soft cheeks, slightly pendulous – were burning red and her expression defiant. He admitted to himself this was not quite the reaction he had sought. He had imagined Betty would be instantly sympathetic and would not allow him to chastise himself. Chastisement was still something he theoretically welcomed but found himself resenting when it began. And now it had begun in earnest. Betty was furious with him. Her words, her tone of voice, had not been particularly violent but her meaning was unmistakable. He felt on the defensive, sullen, irritable that she had automatically attacked him. Perhaps he had simply not explained himself very well.

"Oh, you've explained quite enough," Betty said crossly, and jumping up went across to her typewriter and began pounding away. "I don't want to hear your explanations," she shouted over the noise. "The facts are enough. You're having an affair. It's very commonplace."

"You're being rather narrow-minded, Betty."

"Certainly I am. I thought you were a happily married man and –"

"But I *am*, you've missed the point, I did *say* that I still love Anna and my marriage."

"Rubbish."

"No, I mean it."

"You just want it all ways, that's all. You're a hypocrite. I hope Anna chucks you out. I hope she has the guts to kick you out."

"Betty!"

"Betty nothing. Anyway, Mr Osgood, we shouldn't be talking like this. I'm your secretary. I'm here to work. If we're not going to work I'm going home, now, for good."

Robert rang Claire as soon as Betty had gone for lunch, after an appallingly tense morning. Certainly, they had got through an enormous amount of correspondence but he had a headache with the sheer force of the electricity flashing through the air, generated by Betty's anger. He was so glad when she had gone that he almost collapsed. Then he stirred himself and rang Claire, but they said, at her office, that she had gone away early for the weekend. He felt absolutely livid. It was so inconsiderate of her, so irresponsible. Who else was he supposed to talk to? He rang her flat, hoping to catch her before she left, but there was no reply. There was no other way in which he could contact her.

He sat at his desk bereft of all consolation. The power to live on his own with his own thoughts quite suddenly seemed beyond his ability. How could he ever have contemplated it? He was an utterly woman-dependent man. Anna, Claire, Sarah, even Betty – they were all more independent than he. At different times in this drama which had taken over his life they had all shown themselves able and willing to stand on their own. He admired them. They had a sense of individuality which he did not possess.

Desperately, he looked out of the window. Not a park in sight for him to walk in. Tomorrow, in the country, he would go out and walk miles, perhaps along the nearby river, hoping that the exercise would soothe him. But at the thought of tomorrow the deeper implications of Betty's admission that she *had* posted the letter to Anna, that Anna had received it, that Anna wilfully pretended not to, overwhelmed him. Was the pretence to go on? Was Anna seriously not going to mention it? The idea was grotesque. He simply could not bear the thought of looking Anna in the eye ever again. Shame and panic flooded him. If Anna had cried or sworn, if she had wept or stormed, but not this calm, deliberate deception.

Walking up and down his office, he tried in vain to figure out what it meant. Anna's action must be a kind of code. He must be able to interpret it – there was nothing about her he did not know. Was she condoning his behaviour, saying in effect, "I know but it does not matter"? Was she saying, "I know, but I forgive"? Could she even be encouraging him to carry on as he had been doing? Or was there some deeper meaning he had not even begun to guess at?

Of course, Anna had always had that element of surprise about her. It was wrong to say he knew everything about her. *She* knew everything about him in all the ways that mattered, but he had never quite penetrated an innermost veil of secrecy. There were private areas he had never found the way into. Sometimes it hurt him, saddened him when he was so exposed himself, even made him a little resentful that there were inner sanctums into which he was not privileged to enter. But mostly he had the intelligence to realise that this slim core of reserve about her feelings was a kind of gift Anna gave him. Since she was not entirely predictable, since he did not quite know all, he could never be bored.

They had gone back, last April, to the church in which they had been married by Anna's father, twenty years ago. He was the vicar, then, of the parish of Upper Bothwell in Gloucestershire and the wedding had naturally been in his own church. A pretty wedding, Anna beautiful in a traditional gown. Her father was dead now, her mother long since moved to live with her sister in Wales. They had not been back for fourteen years, not since Harry's christening, the last happy family event before the death of the Rev Mr Dixon. After they had wandered around the churchyard they had gone for a walk along the river, reminiscing about their wedding day, talking quietly about their subsequent luck. Hand in hand, along banks thick with primroses. It was a popular village, a popular walk. They passed one or two other people and said good afternoon. And then, as they turned the bend, at a quiet corner where the river parted but by no means out of possible public view, Anna had pulled him down into the grass and said, "Let's make love." He did not like to think of his own hesitation. Half laughing, half embarrassed, he had joined her in the grass, struggling with his clothes, delighted but disbelieving. The grass was thick and wet but Anna seemed oblivious and he was afraid to admit he was not. All day, afterwards, he had laughed and teased her and she had seemed indifferent to the startling nature of her sudden passion. He would have said, before, that Anna was incapable of spontaneous combustion: everything was always planned. And they had been married twenty years that day, they were long past the stage of being surprised by lust. "Oh yes," Anna said, carelessly, "I planned it. I planned it an hour ago."

Why, with a wife like that, had he needed Claire? He had not needed her, not for sex or love or anything else. Anna had never failed him. He felt he had strayed into the Garden of Eden without knowing it and there he had succumbed to the offer of excess. It was Claire's fault. She had offered herself and he had taken. But *why* had he taken?

Claire claimed total responsibility, it delighted her to see herself as a scheming vamp, but he could not accept this version of what had happened. It took no account of his own response. Again and again he back-tracked in his mind over the actual evening when he and Claire had first slept together. All day she had been at his side, amusing him, diverting him and − yes − attracting him. She had attracted him. It was, it had been, a strong physical attraction. But, once felt, why had he not suppressed it? Because he did not want to. There had seemed no harm in it, he had convinced himself it meant nothing. Then, later, as she slipped her hand into his, the force of his desire had astonished him. He had been afraid of it, and afraid to say he was afraid. It had seemed rude to pull away and reject her − he was so unused to these advances, made so awkward by them. Outside her hotel bedroom door she had said, "Would you like to come in, Robert?" and he had meant to say, "I would *like* to but I mustn't," and only got as far as, "I would like to." He was ashamed of his embarrassment. And he liked her, that was the other factor. She was bold but not cheap. "You needn't *worry*, Robert," she had murmured, "this is just fun, you know, nothing more. You can take it or leave it. Don't be so old-fashioned."

He was old-fashioned. It had never made him feel less of a man but now it did. He was old-fashioned enough to believe in fidelity and now he was unfaithful his system could not absorb the shock. He wanted to tell Anna about it, to explain lust had begun it all, to argue it had come upon him unexpectedly. But then love had entered into it quite quickly and how was he to explain that? He needed to talk to Anna about it. That was why he had precipitated this crisis. He wanted Anna's advice. And he must have it. She could not be allowed to pretend nothing had happened.

Claire had broken the rules. Since the game had changed she hoped they no longer applied. Before she left for Rye, she rang the Osgood household, naturally assuming she would get Anna. Instead, she got a cleaning lady who said Mrs Osgood was out shopping, did she want to leave a message, and then oh, I think I hear her. Claire heard the receiver put down on a table and the exchange of words, too far off to make out.

"Who's that?" another voice said, and quite without thinking Claire replied to the direct question with an equally direct reply.

"Claire Bayley."

"Who do you want?"

"Mrs Anna Osgood, please – but I've already said – it isn't important – I'll ring again."

"Claire Bayley?"

"Yes, but there's no need to say I rang. Please don't bother to give my name. I'd rather just ring again."

"Didn't you work with my father?"

Claire was instantly on her guard.

"Yes. A long time ago."

"Then I know who you are. I'm Sarah, Robert's daughter, the eldest in this family."

Claire imagined a special emphasis on the word "family", a threat implied in it. She said nothing. She planned to get herself off the telephone as quickly as possible.

"Robert told me, if you get my meaning," Sarah said. "I know all about it."

"I don't think we ought to be talking like this, actually. I only wanted to talk to your mother, briefly."

"Why?"

"I think that's my concern."

"Well, you can think again. It's mine too. I don't think my mother wants anything to do with you, I don't know how you have the cheek to telephone."

"I'll ring off now."

"Stop! I just want you to know I won't stand for it – for you doing anything awful to them. I can't spell it out, not with someone else near. But I'm sure you understand – just leave them alone. You don't know what you're destroying."

"I have no intention of destroying anything."

"Then shut up and go away."

"No, I won't."

Claire was astonished at her own stupidity. It was both ridiculous and dangerous to be engaging in this sort of conversation with Sarah Osgood but she had been drawn into it too suddenly to see the outcome. The girl was so rude and aggressive and so – so – so *mistaken* in her crass assumptions.

"I don't think you're old enough to understand –"

"Shit!"

"– what has happened. It isn't my job to tell you. Anyway, I'm sorry to have spoken to you, I should have hung up straight away. I only rang because I was concerned for your mother. I wanted to be sure everything was all right again. That's all. Goodbye."

Sarah put the telephone down. Lily, the cleaning lady, came back into the room and asked if she would give Anna the message or should she write it down as she was supposed to? Sarah snapped that there was no message.

Anna and Gillian did the hospital round together. Gillian pushed the library trolley and Anna handed out the books. The day of the week they did this voluntary work was not inflexible but usually it was a Thursday. By great good fortune it was Gillian who had cancelled Thursday this week and chosen Friday. "I know it isn't convenient," she said to Anna, "with you going to the country. Last thing you want."

"Oh, nonsense," Anna said, "it only takes an hour after all."

They had taken the job on after Imogen's accident, after all the hours and hours at the hospital had revealed to Anna how important auxiliary helpers were. Well, not important so much as welcome. Anyone coming round who was not a doctor or nurse was a diversion, badly needed. So often she had looked up from Imogen's white, still face and seen the bright, bustling, unconcerned faces of the library trolley ladies and the relief had been enormous. Conversation was brisk and banal, a real tonic. They never had any books the remotest bit enterprising – Alistair Maclean for the men, Catherine Cookson for the women – but it didn't matter. Anna hadn't resented them the way she had unreasonably resented the entire medical staff.

On the wards, she remembered her function. Gillian was too obviously sympathetic and concerned. She had never had the opportunity to learn that people in distress or pain, or even people just bored out of their skull, do not really want interested sympathy. Patients in hospital do not have the energy: sympathy is tiring to respond to. What they want is bland cheerfulness, remote and untouching. Anna remembered and was consequently more popular than Gillian, who could not work out why. She thought Anna unfeeling. She never asked patients how they were, Gillian noticed, and she smiled even at those screwed up in agony. It was not somehow right.

They put on their orange overalls – dreadful things but obligatory – and began loading the trolley under the librarian's strict supervision. Surreptitiously, Anna sneaked on to it a few favourite novels, though she had little hope of finding customers for them, and then off they trundled, pleasantly familiar with the route they would take. The Male Surgical Ward was first. Patiently, they put up with the jokes and even the mild, veiled abuse. "I hate doing that ward," Gillian said, the minute they were out. "I hate seeing men in hospital. They look so much worse than women." Quite suddenly and forcefully Anna had a vision of Robert in a hospital bed. She gasped, leant on the trolley. "Anna, whatever is the matter?"

"Nothing. I just – so silly – when you said, about seeing men in hospital, I saw Robert in one of those beds."

"Wishful thinking," Gillian said, complacently.

"*What?*"

"Well, it's obvious, isn't it? You like looking after him, you always have done. If he was in a hospital bed you would be in your element."

"Gillian, that's wicked. How can you say such a thing – I could never, never want Robert helpless in hospital."

"I didn't say that, didn't mean it anyway. What I meant was that whereas I would moan and curse if Doug was in hospital – I mean, I'm a terrible nurse, no patience or tenderness – well, you'd be marvellous, what any man would want. I don't see what's so awful in saying that. You've got that sort of marriage, haven't you?"

Anna was prevented from replying because at that moment they swung into the Orthopaedic Ward, where she was distracted from her indignation at Gillian's statement by a request for "something Russian" from a young man with a dislocated hip. An invigorating discussion on the rival merits of *Dr Zhivago* as opposed to *One Day in the Life of Ivan Denisovich* – the Pasternak was chosen – followed. It was some time before Anna rejoined Gillian.

"You are a flirt, you know, Anna," Gillian said when once

more they were in the corridor. "No, you *are*, but in such a subtle way. You probably don't realise it yourself. I'm sure if you had been the man your marriage would have been quite different. Your Robert never flirts."

For the second time in half an hour Anna was devastated. She put a hand to her forehead, wondering if she had a temperature, wondering if there was some quite simple physical explanation for her vulnerable state. It was not new for Gillian to be blunt. She was renowned for it. But this afternoon the power of her observations seemed formidable. Anna knew she was seeing everything differently because of the events of the last twenty-four hours but even so she was alarmed at her own violent internal reaction to Gillian's blithe comments. She could not laugh (as she would have done last week) and make fun of Gillian in return.

"That's the secret, of course," Gillian was continuing. "That's why your marriage is so stable. You *are* a flirt but you don't know it and so it isn't dangerous. And then you're safely in a home setting and you stay there. It doesn't bore you, like it does Lucy. You're never on the rampage looking for diversion and reassurance like she is. But if you were a man and flirted like you do then some girl would throw herself at you and that would be that. That's what happens to Doug. He doesn't mean to be unfaithful but he can't help flirting, you see, and of course when some poor little flattered girl responds and offers herself he hasn't the heart to say no. Well, at least I understand."

"I don't think you understand at all," Anna said, voice husky with the effort not to shout. "You make it sound as though affairs were an acceptable part of marriage – and as though marriage was just sex."

"Oh no, I didn't say that. I, of all people, I know marriage is *not* just sex. But it's the sex that is the weak link, and if it snaps occasionally I don't see that it matters, not if everything else is strong."

For once Anna felt Gillian might have said something profound. Throughout the Maternity Ward, the Female Surgical, the Dental – throughout all of them she tried out Gillian's bit of folk wisdom on her own case. It would not do. Robert had been at pains in his letter to point out that sex had nothing to do with it. The sex was fine with her, everything was fine. It was just that he now loved both of them. Loved her, loved Claire. That was why he had made his honest declaration. But of course she had not allowed him to make it. So great had been her panic, so deep her cowardice, that she had refused to meet honesty with honesty. She took a deep breath. She ought to talk to Robert.

There was absolutely nobody else to whom she could talk. She found herself experimenting in her head with the idea of it not being impossible to accept the notion of Robert having a mistress so long as otherwise he would be hers. Did it, truly, shock her? If only Robert had not brought love into it – if only he had said it was only sex. But he had not. Was this because he thought it made his affair look more excusable if love was brought into it? Now that she had seen Claire, Anna realised love *did* come into it. She had recognised Claire's attraction. The sudden sexual jealousy she herself had experienced had hurt her – of course, Robert could love this girl. She was lovely. She was quick and clever and original. Anna's bright clear hatred had become muddied by this realisation. She had felt a sense of contact herself. God knew, there were too few people in this world with whom one could feel any sense of identification, male or female, not to acknowledge their existence when they appeared. She had nothing in common with Lucy or Gillian or Elizabeth, nothing but circumstances. Stretching back in time, she could remember so few flashes of recognition. And here there had been one, too late, with the wrong person. Was it conceivable that Robert, she and Claire were all similar? Dared she float such a notion? She wondered what Robert would say, if she gave him the chance to talk about it. This weekend. She had been childish and feeble and even absurd to avoid discussion.

"You're quite right," she said loudly to Gillian, ten minutes later as they approached the Ear, Nose and Throat.

"What about?"

"I forget. But you're right."

Betty was unable to do her shopping for the weekend properly, being blinded by unshed tears. She had planned to start looking for Christmas presents but now, for the first time in her life, there seemed a question-mark over Christmas. When others moaned about the gross commercialisation of this festival Betty had always smiled and felt superior. She liked Christmas. Even in Dundee, where Christmas held no place beside Hogmanay, she had instinctively warmed to the idea of an annual occasion upon which greetings and good fellowship should be spread as widely as possible. She began selecting presents in October and was finished, but for the wrapping and posting, by the first week in December. Yet today, the day chosen for the beginning of her happy shopping, she had no heart for it.

She went and sat instead in a horrible café and stirred a cup of dark orange tea which she had no intention of drinking. Was there anything good left in the world? That, that was the question. In a way, she could only bear not to be happily married herself if she was sure happy marriages existed. She must have something to aspire to. Take away Robert and Anna Osgood's twenty-year-old perfect union and the institution itself became instantly suspect. She could not feel philosophical about it.

Her thoughts turned, in that dreary, steamy, chip-smelling place, to Claire Bayley. She could in truth say she had never liked her. Claire Bayley had never done anything to her during her relatively short sojourn at Gusset and Crowther but she had symbolised all that Betty disliked about the place. But that apart, had Claire Bayley set her cap at Robert? Betty frowned. She would have liked to think this was true but she could not in all honesty say she had ever noticed. Of course, she only saw them in the office building. But Claire Bayley had certainly not been over-frequently in Robert's office and there had been no overt communication between them. Yet it must be that girl's fault. No other interpretation fitted. If she, Claire Bayley, had made the running, did this not provide Robert with a set of extenuating circumstances? He was being childish but perhaps not wicked. A little boy. He had got himself into such a mess.

Betty then thought about Anna and what she had done. Was Anna brave, or misguided? It was so hard to tell. What *should* a wife do when a husband confesses his infidelity? Betty had no idea. She had never been a wife. It had shocked her how confident Robert had been of her understanding, how taken aback he was when she would not give it. Robert clearly thought she worshipped him *unreservedly*. This was not the case. She admired him only for what he was: a happily married man. If he was no longer a happily married man then his identity was gone and her admiration with it. Of course, she still liked Robert – who could not? – but that was a different thing.

Perhaps, as Robert seemed so uncertain where his duty lay, perhaps she ought to have pointed it out to him. Her criticism had not been constructive. She had been angry and upset and disapproving but at no time had she said, "This is what you must do and I will do my best to see that you do it." Would that make a difference to Robert? Betty thought it might. She left the cold tea.

Sarah loathed being in the house with Lily, upon whose plump shoulders rested most of the troubles of the world. Aged fifty-five, Lily had not been fortunate in life. Her first husband beat her, her second was now in prison for receiving stolen goods, a charge which Lily said was only the half of it. She had six children, all of whom had left home as soon as they were earning, except for the youngest, who was unemployed and likely to remain so. Lily was not a treasure. She was slovenly and lazy if not continually watched. Nor did she have a heart of gold. Any extra time was meticulously charged for, regardless of favours done for her. But she had been part of the Osgood household ever since Sarah could remember and was obviously going to remain so.

She was not allowed in Sarah's room. This ought to have pleased her, since she was always looking for excuses to do less, but it perversely annoyed her. She was always trying to sneak in with her wretched Hoover. She made Sarah furious, flicking cigarette ash everywhere in a house where no one smoked, and generally taking short cuts on hard jobs, which Anna then did. Sarah, who never cleaned, liked cleaning to be done properly.

Lily was about to leave. She took off her apron and made a great business of rolling it up and putting it in her bag.

"You can tell your mum," she said to Sarah, whom she disliked as much as Sarah disliked her, "you can tell her I done the top landing like she said only I couldn't get the marks off the carpet. Tried everything but them marks won't budge. Must've been you dropped something."

Sarah did not make the mistake of bothering to deny this allegation. Lily loved arguments.

"Have a nice weekend," she said instead.

"Now that *is* likely, I must say. Trail all the way to Pentonville Saturday, then clean me own place Sunday. Charming. You don't know how the other half live, my girl, with your nice weekends."

"Sorry I spoke," Sarah said, mimicking Lily.

"You might find out one day, that's all. Can't last forever, your lovely life, you'll be out on your neck one fine day, *then* see if you can find a saint like your dad." She waited but Sarah ignored her. "They don't grow on trees, as I know. One in a million, and you have to be something special to get them, like your mum. There now." Still Sarah flicked the pages of her newspaper and said nothing. "I'll be off," Lily said again, belting her coat aggressively. "See your mum Monday."

She banged the door on leaving. Sarah sighed. She no longer challenged Anna on why she put up with Lily – it was a waste of time. Anna was deeply bound up in Lily's troubles, she saw her as a casualty of society. To sack her would be cruel. Sarah had tried to get Anna to see that behind Lily's extravagant adoration of her employers might lie something quite sinister, like contempt. Yet there was something between the two of them – between Anna and Lily – which Sarah could not quite divine. Did Anna need Lily's hero-worship? Was Lily aware of that? Their relationship seemed to Sarah part of the general malaise now affecting her mother's marriage. Anna was not facing facts. Triumphantly, Sarah nodded to herself. She should, after all, be made to.

The Osgoods were watched closely as they packed the car to go to the country. It was a large car, a Peugeot, white and well kept. It stood not quite outside their front door – parking was becoming increasingly difficult in the street, one could never be sure of getting anywhere near one's own patch of kerb – and so the short journey to it, some ten yards from the gate along the pavement, was quite long enough to afford anyone who wanted to see an excellent view of the whole operation.

Lucy did not want to see and yet she could not keep away from her downstairs front window (officially the playroom). The orderliness of the packing filled her with murderous hatred. Everything was so organised. Cardboard boxes of food, neatly covered with gingham tea-cloths; two leather holdalls, presumably full of clothes but as the zips were zipped and nothing gaped Lucy could not be sure; raincoats, on hangers, all ready to lie on top of the luggage; and then a clear space left at the back, with a rug folded exactly to size that fitted it, for the bloody dog.

The human beings were hardly less well arranged. Imogen had been in the car for hours. She appeared to be asleep, her fair head resting in a corner on a cushion. Harry had carried out all the boxes and now stood stroking the dog while Sarah put some small items – books? Lucy could not quite see, though she strained – underneath the seats. Sarah, of course, was a slight flaw in the picture. Lucy regarded her with satisfaction. Harry and Imogen were sensibly and warmly arrayed in jeans and bright pullovers and anoraks and boots but Sarah had on an extraordinary collection of flimsy garments which were hard to sort out. Scarves floated around waist as well as hair and neck and she was bare footed. Her feet must be filthy as well as stone-cold. Lucy saw her go back inside and reappear in a pair of gold lamé high heels before she got into the car, a magazine in hand. Then they all waited. For Robert, obviously. Everything done – Lucy saw Anna literally checking a list – and ready to zoom off as soon as Robert appeared in their second car, a rather bashed up Mini.

Elizabeth passed them as she drove home, to an empty house, an empty weekend. She gave Anna a wave, which was cheerily returned. As she let herself in – it was cold, she was saving on heating now there was only herself to worry about, some weekends – she thought for the thousandth time how much she envied the Osgoods. Not, she hoped, in a horrid way, in a Lucy way. They managed to make the family thing work, that was the point. Even at their happiest, she and Peter had never done that – they had had no sense of corporate identity. Peter sneered at this. He said it was loathsome. He said the Osgoods were no more a perfect family than anyone else, they just looked as if they were. All it took was a determination to image-make. He, Peter, despised image-makers. He liked people who did their own thing and said sod off to what anyone else did.

Well, he had said sod off to her and she was left with wistful dreams of what might have been if she had met and married a Robert Osgood. But then honesty – a freezing kitchen was extremely conducive to honesty – compelled Elizabeth to admit that she was no Anna. She had not worked hard at being a good wife and mother. Perhaps now, in the 1980s, if she had been just starting off, perhaps now it would not have mattered. She had been just fractionally but fatally ahead of her time, putting her career first, admitting work gave her much, much more satisfaction than any other of her roles. The concept of dedicating herself to making a man happy had never really entered her consciousness. But she felt a pang in her heart when she saw a happy family, particularly a family going somewhere or doing something as a unit. How marvellous it must feel, she thought as she filled the kettle, how extraordinarily lucky Anna and Robert are.

Gillian did not say they were lucky. She pushed her youngest home, right past the car and the waiting Osgoods.

"Have a good weekend," she said, nicely, and then, not so nicely, "Rather you than me. I don't know how you can be bothered. Is Imogen asleep?"

"Yes," Anna said, flushing. Gillian knew all about Imogen and why she was asleep.

"Poor love. I suppose it's always going to be an ordeal."

"Let's hope not."

"Robert late?"

"Not really. He can't estimate the traffic, especially on a Friday afternoon."

"Poor man. Doesn't he find it exhausting, jumping out of one car and into another?"

"Yes. But it's so relaxing when we get there."

"Well, I'm glad. Have a nice time."

It was Anna who made it all happen, thought Gillian. She was a funny woman. You could never get really close to her, however friendly she seemed. Always, there was something held back, always Robert was in the way. Sometimes she, Gillian, had gone into the Osgood household in the evening on some errand and she had never failed to come away without the slightly unpleasant feeling that she had intruded. When anyone came to *their* house Gillian knew she and Doug were truly welcoming – they said come in with enthusiasm and urged the visitor to sit down – but the Osgoods were not. They were really quite private. But, unlike Elizabeth, Gillian did not put a favourable interpretation upon this privacy. She wondered instead (though knowing it was rather horrid wishful thinking, not a million miles removed from Lucy's naked jealousy) if the desire to exclude the world did not mean the Osgoods had something to hide.

She saw Robert's Mini coming down the street. He tooted. Anna tooted triumphantly back. He was in and out of the house like a flash. Then off the Osgoods zoomed, leaving the street an emptier place and the spirits of those who had watched their departure strangely deflated.

Seven

Sarah hated the country as much as Imogen loved it. As soon
as they turned off the motorway and the green began she felt
utterly depressed. The raves began from Robert – "Look at
those trees!" – and she wanted to scream. Once, he had
openly pitied his children for not having a country heritage
like Anna and him. He said he felt filled with remorse that
their roots were embedded in London, in concrete and dirt.
She had been furious, had said she felt just as sentimental
about the streets and shops around where they lived as he did
about hills and streams.

Then, when they arrived, Sarah found it so painful to
endure the cries of rapture over every flower and shrub, that
awful ten minutes when Anna and Robert enthused to each
other over the state of the garden. Starving and tired, one
had to wait while they burbled on and then stood in the
porch, facing towards the river below, and said (often in
unison), "Such air! So fresh! So clean!" It was very nearly

insupportable, especially if it was raining.

As the arrival evening wore on, Anna and Robert's pleasure increased by the minute and Sarah marvelled at their innocence. They made her feel so cynical, particularly now, in the light of their little problem. Robert went for a walk with the dog, Anna lit candles for the kitchen table and put the finishing touches to the meal she had brought, Harry lit the fire – more sickly admiring gasps – and Imogen woke up, as surprised as the Sleeping Beauty. All around them, in no time at all, was inky blackness and silence. No good peering out of the window: nothing to see. No good hoping for a doorbell to ring or a telephone: no bell, no telephone. They were two miles from the village and had no friends there anyway. "Just us against the world," Robert always said complacently.

Who wanted to be "just them"? Not Sarah. She kept her head down at supper in case her parents read in her eyes the despair she felt. The candles flickered and drove her mad. "I can't see what I'm eating," she said and jumped up and put on the electric light before anyone could object.

"Oh, not the light!" Anna cried. "It spoils the atmosphere."

And Robert said, "Why do you have to *see* shepherd's pie?"

"To pick out the bits of carrot I don't like," Sarah said.

Of course, Scrabble and Canasta were played. Of course, round the fire. Sarah excused herself, legitimately, on the grounds of homework. Harry was not too keen but without television or snooker he was otherwise lost. With her bad temper for company, Sarah retreated to her room – a mere cell which she had made no attempt to humanise. Her real room was at home in London and she had always remained faithful to it. She sat at the small table under the window with its appalling sprigged curtains and got out her books.

Tomorrow, long walks in Wellingtons, leaves picked, lunch at the pub, garden tidied up, supper, Monopoly . . . Sarah shut her eyes tight for a moment. This inflexible ritual was what she must preserve, even though she hated it, made fun of it. It was too pathetic to think of it being blown sky-high. Twenty years – no, they had only had this cottage since Harry was born – fourteen years of weekends and holidays in the country, ripped away. If Anna and Robert had said to her, "We've decided to give up the cottage," then good, marvellous. "About time," she would have said. But not an abrupt stop. Not Anna, coming on her own with Harry and Imogen. Not Robert, with Claire Bayley.

She tried hard to work but chewed her nails instead. Perhaps she ought to remove Harry and Imogen tomorrow and give Anna and Robert a chance to talk. But they had all night to do that, if they wanted. They always sat up late in the country, oohing and aahing over the bloody fire. They had no need of any other time. That is, if they got down to it, if they did not shirk their duty. It would be quite terrible if the whole wretched weekend went by and *nothing was said*. Monday would bring Claire Bayley telephoning again and she, Sarah, would not be there to intercept. Please God they would talk it out tonight.

Harry went to bed first. "Nothing else to do," he said. "Might as well." But Imogen stayed, remarkably bright and cheerful. Neither Anna nor Robert wished to drive her away by hinting that she should go to bed too. Anna had a theory that the reason why neither she nor Robert was particularly close to Sarah was that they had shown too clearly, at an early age, that they liked to be alone. Even if they were just reading, on either side of the sitting room, they did not like being interrupted. It was a shameful admission. Sarah was a sensitive, highly intelligent girl, Anna said, and she had sensed she was not always welcome. It had been their fault and Anna was determined not to let the same thing happen with Harry and Imogen.

Now, the logs burning beautifully, Anna took up her knitting. It was only a scarf, only a sort of running joke that she should knit in the country. Robert got out his stamps and peered at them with his magnifying glass, Stanley Gibbons catalogue to hand. Another country pastime, another half-joke, but with a more serious basis. Imogen sat on a stool, just staring into the fire, but not soulfully, thank God. Occasionally, she prodded a log with the poker, which both Anna and Robert found annoying but they said nothing. There was no harm in it. Anna would rather have seen Imogen gainfully employed, knitting or sewing or drawing, for her own sake, but she was not going to push it. There was daydreaming and daydreaming: she had learned, with Imogen, to recognise when it was dangerous and when it was beneficial. But she did feel bound to say, at eleven o'clock, when for nearly two hours Imogen had sat without moving, "Imo, darling, I don't want to nag, but don't you think you need to go to bed?"

"I'm not tired. I hate going to bed."

Anna's needles clicked. She made a performance of sorting out her wool. Not only did she not want to look Imogen in the eye – the pain was too real – but she did not want to look Robert in the eye. She was afraid of that intimacy she had always loved.

"I might go to bed myself," Robert said. "I *am* tired. It's been . . ." He was going to say a hard week, but stopped. Rather awful to say that. There was a certain awkwardness about leaving Anna and Imogen by the fire too. "It *is* late, you know," he said, not wanting to be the one who left, who broke up the circle. He could not work out whether Anna was using Imogen as an excuse, a shield, or whether she wanted to come with him to bed but did not wish to appear to desert her daughter.

"All right," Imogen said suddenly. "I'll go. But I won't sleep, I know I won't."

"You will. You always do in the country, remember?"

He was in bed first, uncertain whether to leave the lamp on or off. Anna went with Imogen and stayed long enough for Robert to be genuinely almost asleep, but he jerked himself awake as Anna got into bed. Were they going to talk, or not? If they were, he would rather be beside the fire.

"She has such awful dreams, still, night after night. It seems such a dreadful fate for a child, every night knowing what lies ahead."

"That's a bit morbid."

"I feel morbid."

"It's the autumn, usual thing, everything dying and all that."

It was not just the autumn. Robert saw the opening and so did Anna. What else is dying, has died, she wanted to say. Everything changes, that's all, he could reply, then it grows again, nothing has really disappeared. But he was silent, and so was she. There was too much to say ever to begin, surely that was the truth.

Sarah stayed in bed all morning, even though the sun streamed through the curtains. Long ago, she had been up with them at seven on a day like this and off riding before breakfast but now the sole perk of Saturday morning was an uninterrupted lie in bed. No attempt was made to get her up to join the jolly fun. She smelled coffee and then drifted off to sleep again and when she was wakened by them all trooping into the stone-flagged kitchen below she smelled bacon. They would all be pink-cheeked and glowing. Any minute there would be more noise as they excitedly left for The Walk.

Slowly, Sarah got up. Might be a scrap of bacon left. She pulled on the jeans and jumper always left here – otherwise she would get nagged – and trailed downstairs.

"Marvellous morning," Robert said.

"And it's going to be a lovely day," Anna added. Sarah saw them both smile, but not quite at each other.

"I was thinking," she said, "you might let me drive the car around. I could take Harry and Imogen for a run some-where."

"*Big* deal," Harry said.

"You're better off in the Mini," Robert said firmly.

"Such a *lovely* day," Anna said, "it seems a shame to get in a car at all. And you know that Imogen –"

"*I* don't want 'a run'," said Imogen, contemptuously.

"Great," Sarah said. "Fine. I just thought it would give you two some time to yourselves, to sort things out. But never mind."

Heart thudding, Anna became a whirlwind of activity. Of course, all Sarah had meant by "to sort yourselves out" was literally that – to tidy the kitchen, the garden, to decide what to take back to London and what to leave, to get on with the ceremonial shutting-up-for-the-winter of the cottage. But Robert looked stunned. He stared after Sarah's retreating back as though he had seen an unpleasant vision. Anna was terrified he would make a remark that would reveal every-thing. He might think that she *had* got his letter (though Betty had promised), he might think she had told Sarah, he might think all sorts of things when she very badly wanted him not to think at all, not yet. (When? Not *yet*.) So she began to burble on, about putting the Frostat on and up-ending the mattresses near the radiators (everything got very damp) and emptying the cupboards of every scrap of food. She just wanted to to be busy, very busy, and she wanted Robert to be busy too. Most of all, she wanted them both to enjoy this last weekend. Everything else must come second to that. Nothing must spoil the pattern.

Claire was not meanwhile enjoying her weekend. Her mother was irritating, her father hardly less so. They were pleased to see her, made much of her, but they were not exactly kindred spirits. She seemed to have to repeat most remarks twice and even then an all-enveloping bland smile was the most likely response. She wondered if it was absolutely normal or an indictment of their whole relationship that she could not even consider discussing Robert with them. What advice could they possibly give her? How could they help? And they would react to the story of Anna's visit with absolute horror – the sheer vulgarity of it would appal them.

Claire wondered, as, like Robert and Anna some hundred miles away, she walked and walked on Saturday afternoon, whether what she was feeling was concealed guilt. She had never thought of everything being brought out into the open, never contemplated anything so startlingly melo-dramatic as a showdown. When she had walked into Robert's life she had simply thought she would have him and damn the consequences. The whole point of being just twenty-two was that one could damn consequences freely since so few of them were yours. Claire suspected there was a good deal of the masochist in her make-up, or perhaps what used to be called masculine drive. She couldn't bear men who were easy to get. Any man who made advances she was automatically not interested in. Quite literally she felt her ardour cooling towards some attractive man if he made it clear he found her attractive too – and most of them did if they felt they had half a chance. She liked to make the running herself. The harder the challenge, the more she relished it. And Robert had been *such* a challenge, so deeply rooted in his happy marriage.

I have been deceitful, thought Claire, imagining that because I had no intention of breaking Robert's marriage it was therefore all right to go ahead. She suddenly saw her behaviour as an act of emotional vandalism. But that admitted, she was nowhere nearer deciding what to do. She had promised Anna to help Robert go back on his decision to live by himself because he was dishonouring his marriage. She had sent him back home − indeed, delivered him − but she was not so naïve as to suppose the case rested there. Robert would be struggling. It would be so tempting for him to carry on as usual, aided and abetted by Anna, Claire and Betty. But surely Anna knew Robert? Surely she saw this simply would not do?

Besides, Claire conceded to her stern inner self, I have changed. She had surely been fooling herself to imagine she could be happy if Robert disappeared from her life. Such an attitude had been bravado, cocking a snook at herself. She missed Robert, better to admit it. Things had not gone quite how she had thought they would. She looked back over the last few months and saw herself cheating. Because she had known she could not be serious about Robert she had assumed she never would be. Robert's marriage was such a useful screen behind which to hide her own feelings. Now he had whipped that screen away and she was not sure that she could stand the sudden exposure. Could she truthfully say goodbye to Robert, tell him, as she had done at the beginning, that it was just "fun"?

Robert conquered was no longer so easy to set aside. Was what she now, to her own surprise, felt for him love? It certainly was not lust; how quickly lust was satiated. If that were all, it was over, done, settled down into a satisfying but bearable pleasure. "You don't know," Anna had said, "what Robert means to me. You couldn't possibly understand what there is between us. I can't put it into words, but it's there." Yes, Claire thought, it is there, for me too. But Anna was there first. There were two souls waiting for Robert when he was born and Anna got there first, twenty years early. So the decent British thing to do was to be a good loser.

I am not a loser, Claire thought, mud up to her knees. I don't believe in fair play and better luck next time. Now that I have been forced to see there is a fight on, I'll fight.

Betty looked through the Situations Vacant columns on Saturday. She could go anywhere, whenever she liked. Good shorthand and typing, experience, excellent references – she had no fears. If things came to the worst, as they appeared to be going to do, she could hand in her notice and not have to worry about another job. But a warmth would go out of her life and she knew she needed it.

All Saturday, she cleaned her tiny flat. Betty was what the Americans call a home-maker. She loved decorating and cleaning and spent hours refurbishing her belongings. Most of her weekends were taken up hunting through markets and junk shops for second-hand furniture, which Betty re-upholstered herself. She had a Welsh dresser which she had stripped herself, revealing beautiful oak, and on its shelves were plates of green and white china – *green* and white, most unusual, very hard to collect. She had sanded her own floors and polyurethaned the boards and she had even made her own rug, at evening classes. One day she intended to have a whole house, just a little one, in Chelsea or Fulham. She could not work towards *someone* to love her but she could towards *something*.

Robert had been in her flat only once, to collect her on one occasion when she was going with him to a conference. She had let him come in while she made a pretence of finding her coat. He had been very taken with her flat, complimented her on so many things, and yet he had not been at ease and neither had she. Seeing Robert there, standing in the middle of her living room, Betty had suddenly seen how feminine her home was. A man did not fit in. The room was revealed as too tidy, too cluttered, too precisely formal. She felt painfully embarrassed, as though she had taken her clothes off and made an exhibition of herself. She had hustled Robert out and held it against him that he had been inside at all.

Often, Betty had fantasised Robert putting his arms around her. It was a harmless fantasy, surely? Betty was so used to denying herself luxuries that she was almost afraid to indulge herself even in her dreams but this way she did. Only arms, nothing more – only affectionate tenderness. She did not feel any disgusting physical thrill, it was not mental masturbation. She just, in her fantasy, felt comforted and happy. Robert's arms made her feel happy. So she supposed that, in a way, she might be feeling jealous now that she knew Robert's arms had actually been round Claire Bayley. If Claire, it could have been Betty. Why *not* her? Because Robert did not find her attractive, obviously. But he had not found Claire attractive. A conversation came back clearly to Betty, a conversation in which Robert had said, of the new Miss Bayley, "Beautiful? Really? I never noticed. But she's certainly bright." So Robert had gone for her mind, except that Betty conveniently remembered another conversation. "Clever? Yes, I suppose so. I can't say I like that sort of cleverness much. Doesn't get you anywhere really." Well, it had got Claire Bayley a long way. Robert must either have been lying or there was some other vital factor she, Betty, was missing.

On Sunday, Betty went and bought some material and began making some cushion covers just to keep herself occupied. Thinking about Robert and Claire was making her feel ill. It was sick, she must stop it. She was so disappointed – again and again that was what she came back to. But all that long Sunday – she had toasted crumpets at half past four – she was haunted by the unpleasant realisation that her infatuation for Robert and Anna, for their marriage, had always been unhealthy. She should *never* have admired Robert so much. He was only human. She had set him on a pedestal and who knew what possible damage this excessive hero worship had caused? The world wished to knock you down if you were up on a pedestal. Robert had not asked (nor had Anna) to be elevated to such dizzy heights. They themselves had not claimed perfection: it was others who thrust it upon them and she had been one of them.

Yet, Betty concluded as she prepared for bed, I did think they were perfect. "Nothing is wrong with Anna, with Anna and me," Robert had stressed. She did not believe it. If she wanted to help Robert, and in spite of everything she did, then that was the way to do it: make him confess something had been lacking or Claire Bayley, however persistent, could never have got a hold on him.

On Saturday night Sarah knew they still had not talked. Robert was hearty, Anna hardly less so. The tension was still unmistakably there. She wanted to bang their stupid heads together – both of them were mishandling this. There was nothing to be done about Anna – it was too great a betrayal to confront her with the news that she knew about the letter – but Robert was a different matter. He had it coming to him.

"Dad," she said, on Sunday morning when Anna was already obsessed with a final packing, "let's go for a walk."

"I'll come," Imogen said.

"No, it's private. You can go with him when we get back. Robert loves walking, he'd love two walks, come on, Dad."

He had no option. Stiff with loathing for such un-accustomed exercise, Sarah walked with Robert along the tow-path of the river.

"I'm not walking far," she said after a few yards. He looked so hunted, muffled up in a scarf and horrible cap. "I only want to know what's going on. What *is* going on?"

"Nothing." He pawed at the ground; everything about him was suddenly feeble and infuriating.

"Well, don't you think there should be?"

"I'm not going to tell you not to interfere –"

"Good. *You* dragged me into this."

"I knew you'd say that. I know I did. Of course, I wish I hadn't, naturally –"

"But you came back, Thursday night, as though nothing had happened."

"It hadn't. Betty said she hadn't posted that letter I told you about."

"So Anna never got it? You mean she doesn't know, you needn't tell her? *What* an escape – you lucky bugger."

"Hang on. On Friday Betty said she *had* posted it. Anna asked her to say she hadn't, you see, so she did, then she thought better of it –"

"You mean, Anna *does* know?"

"Yes."

"But she's not saying she knows?"

"At least you're quick, Sarah."

"But this is gross – it's painful – why haven't you spoken to Mum, then?"

"She doesn't want me to."

"You're a coward."

"I am, but it isn't that. She doesn't want to talk, about anything. She just wants to carry on as though nothing has happened."

They walked on. Robert supposed it was the ultimate in

humiliation. If only Sarah had laughed at the absurdity of it all but she looked grim, was actually walking quickly in her confusion. He was almost frightened when she abruptly stopped after half a mile and swung round on him.

"Well, you've had your lesson," she said fiercely. "It's enough, isn't it? I presume you won't see this Claire character again. I mean, in all decency you couldn't, could you? Not after what Mum's been through?"

"That's not what you said two days ago."

"Dad, that was before I knew Anna knew. Now it's quite clear. You just give up Claire, fast, and forget it. You weren't made for affairs, you're just incapable of handling them."

"Claire wasn't an affair."

"Bloody hell!"

"It was her – as a person – like with Anna, with your mother – the same contact. It was nothing to do with sex or anything."

"They all say that. Of course it was to do with sex. It always is. And boredom. You were just bored but you didn't even realise it. It's pathetic."

"I was *not* – am *not* – bored!" shouted Robert all the way down the river. "I love my marriage, I love my wife."

There weren't any thick clouds of leaves on the trees down by the river to muffle the sound. Robert stood, red in the face, his arms spread wide, appealing to the cold blue sky, not to Sarah. He felt a great surge of confidence just from saying those words aloud. "It isn't impossible, you know," he said more quietly.

"It's impossible being *you*," Sarah said, but she was impressed. "Can't you imagine what people would think?"

"I don't care what anyone thinks."

"Yes, you do. You have to. You don't lead the sort of life where you can afford not to. And Mum, what about her, she would certainly have to care. What would Gillian and Lucy and Elizabeth think? You'd crucify her if it came out."

"You, of all people," Robert said bitterly, "putting these arguments, throwing convention at me. I've never said *you* shouldn't behave as you do because of what people would think. Anna and I just put up with what they think and we haven't enjoyed it."

"I'm eighteen, Dad. It's different. I haven't got a marriage to uphold."

"I don't think you ever will have. It doesn't seem worth anything to you, to your generation."

"To *your* generation. The only good marriage I knew was your marriage and now look at you."

"You're cruel, Sarah. And not even thoughtlessly."

"I'm not cruel. I'm angry, furious."

"I can't think why. You've always despised Anna and me for being cosy and suburban. You ought to be pleased."

"Dad, you're so stupid, *cretinous*. You can't seem to see what's in front of your nose. You're absolutely obsessed with your own thoughts, your feelings, your worries – you don't even see anybody else's. What right have you got to be so aggrieved? None, bloody none. It's Mum who's wronged and there she is, fighting away, helping you by keeping everything normal."

"Helping? She won't face facts."

"Fuck bloody facts."

"We've walked far enough," Robert said, turning, gazing sightlessly up the tow-path. He hated Sarah. He needed Anna to protect him from this ruthless daughter. "Imogen will be waiting. And this shouting match isn't getting us anywhere. We might as well stop."

"*I'm* not stopping. I'm carrying straight on until you come to some conclusion. That's a definite threat. And I've got another. If you don't make your mind up soon I'll go and see Miss Claire Bayley and point out a few things to her – a few of your precious facts."

"Don't be so silly, Sarah."

"I've already spoken to her anyway."

"I don't believe you."

"She rang up on Friday. I gave her a piece of my mind."

"You're lying, not that it matters. Claire would never ring up."

"She rang up for Anna, for Mum. Lily answered, just as I was coming in."

Robert slowly began walking back the way they had come. He felt sick. Claire rang Anna? Lily answered, then Sarah. So she had not spoken to Anna. Thank God. There was sweat on his brow. Sarah grimly shadowed him, almost taller in her unaccustomed Wellingtons.

"There's six hours before we go home, Dad," she said. "You've got six hours to decide what to do, once and for all."

Anna, always strong and energetic, was exhausted. The strain of packing up for the winter was too great. Not just the physical strain of so much clearing up and packing away, but the emotional strain of being forced into the position of thinking, "I wonder what will have happened by the time we open this cottage up again." She was unfortunately given to that sort of sentimental rambling anyway. Sometimes there had been such enormous events ahead it was justifiable to wonder aloud – "Will it be a boy or girl by the spring, Robert?" . . . "Will you be a director by March, Robert?" . . . "Will father be better?" . . . "Will Imogen be her old self?" Sometimes she had to keep very quiet, when the thoughts were too awful, like now. So she worked away furiously and had no time to enjoy the last of the autumn sunshine.

Everyone else did, particularly Imogen. She came back

from her walk with Robert glowing with health and smiling too, quite boisterous in fact. "I wish we could live here forever," she said.

"Maybe one day," Robert said.

"We've always intended to live in the country," Anna said, "when it's possible, when Robert's head of Gusset and Crowther."

"If I were head of Gusset and Crowther I'd have to be in London even more than I do now. It isn't a soft option, being head of the firm."

"Mr Crowther makes it one."

"But I wouldn't be a George Crowther."

"Anyway, I wish we could," Imogen said. "Now."

"Why exactly?" Anna pressed, but knowing.

"It's so safe," Imogen said and blushed.

"And boring," Harry broke in.

"I like life being boring. I just want it to be boring, nothing awful ever happening."

"Nothing nice or exciting either," Harry said. "Nothing ever happens here that I can see."

"Exactly," Imogen said. "I like nothing happening."

Anna was startled to find tears in her eyes. She rushed off to put blankets in moth-balls and frowned hard as she mounted the stairs. Quite, quite awful to remember that once she had contemplated using that sort of blackmail. One could not use children, it was much too dangerous. Even worse was the realisation that as Imogen spoke a voice at the back of her mind was saying that if Robert left she would sell this cottage. It was the first time she had admitted the possibility and she was horrified at the way in which her brain at least seemed to be adjusting so practically to disaster.

She knew of course that Robert was trying to talk to her. Everywhere she went he followed, would-be helpful. He was constantly suggesting they both needed to do vital jobs in the most inaccessible parts of the large garden. But she side-stepped all his appeals. She knew now for certain that she was not going to talk to him after all. The resolution of Friday had weakened as soon as Robert had got in the car beside her: his actual presence, his very flesh, was an insurmountable barrier to rational thought. She had, this weekend, gone past worrying about her strong desire for evasion. She *wanted* to evade discussion – it was an urgent need, there was no point in questioning this basic primitive urge to pretend. Not for one minute did she think her attitude was "right", she could not defend it, but it was stronger than reason. Once certain words had passed between them she was absolutely convinced all would be lost.

And there was something the matter with Sarah. She too pursued Anna, though in a different way. She suggested Anna should go for a last walk with Robert, that she would see to the final packing of the car, and when Anna politely declined this unusual offer of help Sarah said, "Oh *Mother*,' in her most exasperated tone and was clearly angry. She was on the edge of almost violent impatience all afternoon. "*Mother*," she kept saying, "you're wasting the afternoon. It's ridiculous. For God's sake relax, make the most of it. What does it matter about the bloody cupboards?"

"It matters a great deal," Anna said primly. "If I come back in March and find five hundred mice have taken over because I left half a biscuit stuck somewhere it would matter a lot."

"There are things you'd care about more than mice, I presume."

Anna did not ask Sarah what she meant, any more than she would have asked Robert. She was scared, did not want to know what Sarah meant. There was no doubt that Sarah had in some strange way cottoned on to something. Quite what, she did not like to think but the clues were too thick on the ground to be ignored. Usually, Sarah lived her own life exclusively, taking little interest in family doings. This weekend was in itself amazing and Anna now appreciated she ought to have regarded Sarah's willingness to come with the greatest suspicion. She did not really want Sarah's sharp little mind ticking over, observing acutely and putting two and two together. Harry and Imogen were different, they were a unit, but Sarah's maturity posed problems, it always had done. She could not be hoodwinked. Anna supposed, as she did the last bit of sweeping out, that Sarah would side with Robert, when the truth was out. (*When?* Another slip of the mind.) She would understand. Sarah could be Claire herself.

At last, it was over. Cottage locked securely, the shuttered windows giving it a sad, blinkered look. One key deposited under the black stone in the orchard wall where their nearest thing to a friend and neighbour knew where to find it in an emergency. They were all in the car, vital belongings checked. Imogen had refused sedation, was sitting bravely in the back next to Anna. Sarah sat with Robert. They seemed, Anna thought, not to be speaking – they had had some row.

"Well," Robert said as they drove down the lane, "that was a nice weekend."

"Bloody waste of time," Sarah said.

"Oh Sarah," Anna said, "don't say that. You might not have got anything out of it but we did."

"*You* did?" Sarah said scornfully. "It was you who wasted this weekend most of all, next to Dad."

Eight

"I was wondering," Betty said when she went into Robert's office on Monday morning (he looked gratifyingly normal again), "if we could have lunch together. I've never suggested it before because you know I can't afford it. But I would like you to have lunch with me, Robert, please." It was amazing how casually she managed to come out with it. If Robert guessed she had practised and practised she would be very, very surprised.

"I'd be delighted, Betty," Robert said, with his nice smile. "Any special reason? You know I'm rotten at birthdays and things."

"I'll tell you at lunch."

Of course, Robert was not delighted. He wanted to see Claire. The family weekend, instead of making the image of Claire fade, had only made it larger. Claire had *not* gone right out of his life and she was not going to. Confrontation with Anna had not taken place and that was not going to happen either. And he was not leaving home. That was the sum total of his decision-making to date and he wished to inform Claire of it without delay. He also wanted to express his concern and astonishment that she had rung Anna. Why? It terrified him more every time Sarah's words — oh God, *Sarah* — came back to him.

She rang him at half past eleven, to his great pleasure. He had not been able to ring her, he explained, because of Betty, who had stuck doggedly in the office all morning. When he said, "Oh, hello," (Betty did not answer the phone if she was typing) Betty got up and immediately went out, shutting the door, to Robert's immense relief. He had not known his voice conveyed so much information.

"Darling," he said at once, "thank God — I went crazy on Friday when I couldn't get you — where were you?"

"I went home. To think. Away from your evil influence."

"I was away anyway."

"Robert, I need to see you."

"*I* need to see *you*."

"What about lunch?"

"I can't. I'm having lunch with Betty."

"Lunch with Betty?"

"I know, but she asked. We had a bit of a row on Friday — I'll tell you later — anyway, I can't let her down. It will have to be after work. How about at the National, about five?"

"Robert, we don't need that sort of thing any more. Just come to my office, pick me up, we'll go back to my flat."

"It's a bit —"

"Robert, the rules have changed, you changed them, remember? I won't play the old game. I'm tired of it. No subterfuge. If you're seen, you're seen. I'm still not breaking your marriage but I'm not hiding either and I'm not helping you to hide. I don't like ultimatums, they're absurd, but if you don't just turn up, as anyone else would, then I'll know you can't take it."

"Claire, you —"

"Robert, I'm not going to argue on the telephone. Understood? I'll see you or I won't see you. 'Bye."

"You look absolutely exhausted," Gillian said severely. Anna gave her a wan smile. "I can't see a weekend in the country does you any good at all if you come back looking like this."

"It was packing up for the winter. It wasn't a typical weekend. It just *is* tiring."

"I saw you coming back, laden."

"I've got some apples for you. I'll bring them in. And some beech leaves, if you want them. Did you have a nice weekend?"

"Lovely. Doug didn't come home at all on Friday night, absolutely charming start to any weekend. Arrived midday on Saturday looking shattered with some cock-and-bull story about missing a train. Really, I said to him, why pretend, it was obvious he'd spent the night with somebody – that's what annoys me, the pretence. It's so insulting."

Gillian sat down in Anna's kitchen without being asked, her coat still on, the shopping bags dangling from her plump red wrists. Coffee was expected and given, though Anna was impatient for peace. She knew Gillian was set for the best part of an hour and that there would be no escaping the tirade against her husband which Anna found so embarrassing. She wanted to tell Gillian that she knew this assumed anger was all a kind of inverted boasting – she was actually proud of Doug's escapades, only pretending to be furious. She thought she was open and honest and that all the world should be like her.

Yet as Anna listened she found herself so in need of

comfort and advice that once more there stole over her that dangerous longing to confide, this time in Gillian – big, comfortable, broad-minded Gillian, who would love it, who would dab up her misery like a great pad of fluffy cotton wool. Anna closed her eyes momentarily and told herself no. It would not be worth it. Gillian would be genuinely concerned but thereafter she would never let go, never. There would be breathless daily enquiries, whispered solicitous questions. And what would be the good? How could Gillian, knowing nothing of Anna's sort of marriage, help? From her vantage point the view was clear, but it was not Anna's. The humiliation would be awful, not just from the shame of being a wronged wife (a role with no glory) but from revealing her own crying need for reassurance.

So Anna struggled, successfully, and when she surfaced again heard that Gillian had moved on from marital infidelity of one sort to another.

"Well, I had her to lunch," she was saying. "I just could not bear to think of her on her own in that gloomy house all weekend. I admit, she was reluctant, I had to practically force her. We had Doug's cousin Ned here, you see, and he's just Elizabeth's type. They got on so well. I wouldn't be surprised if Ned took her out – he was very keen."

"I thought he was married?"

"Oh he is, but in name only. They agreed, you know, for the sake of the children, not to part officially till the youngest is sixteen. It seems absurd to me but they're quite happy, they both go their own ways and it seems to work very well. Everything goes on as normal but each gets what they want and no questions asked." Gillian stopped, frowned. "Really, Anna, you do look *awful*. What *is* the matter? I wish you would tell me instead of just sitting looking like death."

"I wish I could, but I can't. I mean, I can't because there

isn't anything to tell, there isn't anything the matter. I'm just tired."

"I hope that *is* all. Nothing worrying you?"

Gillian's large, calm blue eyes held Anna's gaze so steadily that Anna felt a blush rising in her cheeks and alarm in her heart. She was saved by Sarah coming to say she was off. "Bye, Mum. Back late today, remember."

"Good heavens, ten o'clock," Gillian said. "What a time to start school," and gave her silly, high-pitched, affected laugh.

Sarah ignored her, took an apple, went.

"She looks well anyway," Gillian said, sniffing. "I'm glad somebody benefited from your weekend. Actually some colour in her face for once, though don't think I'm getting at you. I know she's eighteen, you're not her keeper exactly. I saw her with that Tom last week. Is he the latest?"

"Yes. They've been friendly for quite a while."

"*Friendly* – I should think they're more than that. I hope you don't mind me asking, Anna, but is she on the pill?"

"I don't know."

"Don't you think you should? I'm not a prude, you know – I mean, the pill is there to be used. It was meant for girls like Sarah. God knows, if we'd had the pill when we were teenagers things might have been very different, for all of us. It was just too late, wasn't it? I would never have got married that first time if the pill had existed, never, not so young anyway. It's changed marriage, hasn't it. Hasn't it, Anna?"

"Has it? I don't know."

"Of course it has. Even for us. All that fretting about getting pregnant. Think how it would have affected our marriages even now, especially now, at forty plus with the menopause coming up and never knowing from one month to another where we were – *think* of having to worry about having a baby at forty-five. Dear God, it would have killed me. How could our mothers have had any kind of spontaneous sex life? Well, they couldn't. You must admit, Anna, we *all* benefit from the pill, Anna, don't we? Even you and Robert, you couldn't be nearly so happy without the pill? Anna?"

Anna felt faint. Gillian's voice, though shrill, seemed a long way off. And then deliverance came a second time with the arrival of Lily, moaning and groaning.

"I'd better be going," Gillian said, reluctantly. "Now I'm going to Sainsbury's tomorrow, Anna — would you like to come?"

"Sainsbury's? No, I don't think so. I don't need anything."

"Don't you? It's two weeks since you've been," Gillian said, aggrieved. "I would have thought you *did* need to go."

"Morning, Mrs Deakin."

"Good morning, Lily. I'm just going. I've been telling Mrs Osgood she doesn't look well."

"I can see she doesn't. She looks as bad as I feel."

"Have some coffee, Lily," Anna said. "I'll leave you to it. I've got to go out."

"Out?" Gillian said.

"Yes."

"Where?"

It was too much. Neighbourly interest and concern yes, but not this taking over of one's life.

"I'm meeting Robert for lunch," Anna lied.

"Good heavens, you've only just seen him off to work," Gillian said, crossly.

"They're love-birds, them two," Lily said. "You won't find the like anywhere else. Can't get enough of each other. Marvellous, innit, Mrs D? You've got to admit, now haven't you?"

Robert felt awkward going out for lunch with Betty, which

was silly, he knew – he'd taken Betty out for lunch often and never felt the least bit awkward. But Betty assumed the role of leader in such a determined fashion that Robert felt like a displaced person.

"Red or white?" Betty said, sternly.

"Either. I don't have to have wine, Betty, really."

"I want wine. Red? Right. And we'll have two home-made soups, then spinach quiche and salad. Thank you."

"This is a treat," Robert said, then quailed at Betty's expression.

"It might as well be," Betty said. "It might be the last lunch we'll have together. I might as well say straight out – I'm thinking of handing in my notice."

"Oh Betty, really, this is crazy, just because –"

"It isn't 'just'. It's everything, no, let me say my say. I love you, Robert, you know that perfectly well."

Robert hiccuped, mopped his mouth, out of which red wine dribbled, swallowed, coughed, gasped and said, "Oh my God, I don't know what to say."

"You don't have to say anything, you'll be pleased to hear. Of course, I love you but I don't mean in a sexual way."

Robert looked round in panic. Betty was delivering her incredible message with the fervour and voice-projection of an evangelist. There was no attempt at tearful intimacy, for which he ought to be grateful. The loud, firm tone Betty was adopting desensitised her words and yet alarmed him unduly.

"Betty," he whispered, "my dear, please –"

"What I've always loved about you, Robert, no, please do not interrupt, is your niceness and your honesty and you being happily married. I don't think you're nice any more and you haven't been honest and you're no longer happily married."

"But I am, Betty, really I am."

"No you're not. It takes two people to be happily married and Anna isn't happy, not since last week. What did you say to her this weekend? About me telling you I had posted the letter? About me betraying her? I suppose she hates me?"

"I didn't mention it. There wasn't an opportunity."

"So you let her go on imagining you didn't know she'd got your letter?"

"I suppose so."

"Why?"

"I couldn't think what else to do. She seemed to want it that way. It's hard to describe, Betty. Anna and I have been married so long, things just continue – I can't explain – our marriage marches on on its own, we don't have to do anything to make it. We get carried along, especially in emergencies. Remember Imogen's accident? You said – everyone said – how could we go on as normal during that time when she might have died, but it wasn't hard, things just ticked over, we just did the same things in the same way, there's a sort of momentum."

"Still?"

"Still. In fact, especially now. It's the saving grace of the whole situation. I'd need energy to stop the marriage; I don't need it to go on with it. And of course I want to go on with it. I'd die without it."

He seemed to have successfully side-stepped Betty's declaration of love. He saw, across the table, that she was not sitting quite so straight and her eyes were no longer glazed. She was absorbed in what he was telling her, just as she had always been. He steadied himself, took a deep breath.

"Betty, I want to ask you again, what do you think I should do?"

"Give up Claire Bayley," Betty said, promptly. "At once, now. Never see her again."

"I can't."

"Yes you can, Robert. If she loves you she'll agree."

"Self-sacrifice isn't her line."

"You don't surprise me. But she's intelligent and sensible. What's the alternative? You won't leave Anna, Anna wouldn't let you continue as you are."

"She might. She seems to me to be telling me, in a way, that she might, that she understands."

"But *you* said you couldn't. That's how this awful business started, about your absurd letter."

"Perhaps I'll have to learn. If I thought Anna could bear it."

"You'd *let* her bear it?"

"I suppose I would. It would be cruel, but —"

"It would be monstrous. And it would destroy your marriage, whatever you say."

"Oh God," Robert said, "what do other people do? I really would like to know. I didn't ask for this to happen, I didn't want it to happen, but it has happened and I can't go back on it."

Surprisingly, they ate. They both cleared their plates with great rapidity. Betty marvelled at the fact that she was enjoying herself, that it could be possible. She wondered if Robert had even heard her say she loved him. When she had finished her wine, she smiled at him. She suddenly felt sophisticated.

"You and I, Robert," she said, "have always been naïve in life, don't you think? Shouldn't we change? Do we have to be such puritans?"

Claire worked hard all day, almost in a feverish way. She took no lunch. As the afternoon wore on she watched the clock anxiously. She intended to make no concessions: she would remain literally at her desk until well after five o'clock and then she would leave by the back entrance just in case Robert was trying to cheat by hanging about in the street. She wished to make a point of being publicly claimed.

Even that would achieve nothing, it was only a matter of principle. Who knew Robert Osgood in James and James? Very few people. He had no distinguishing features – he had no beard, was not noticeably either too large or small, had neither a stammer nor a lisp, nor even a particularly remarkable accent. Everyone who was anyone in publishing knew him but not the secretaries and typists at James and James. Who was there to tell tales to Anna? Who did Anna know? Nobody. Robert's visit, if he made it, would pass without comment. He was self-important if he did not see that. It was not as though *she* were returning to Gusset and Crowther. Now that would be different, very. The beady-eyed Betty, who knew her, who knew Anna, would make capital out of her knowledge. It would be a far greater test of Robert's resolution to announce she was coming to collect him. Claire wished she had thought of it, but recollected that it would have been false. She would never go out to Wandsworth in the ordinary course of events and that was the point: by coming to collect her she wanted Robert to see she was only requiring him to do what was natural and ordinary.

The phone rang constantly during the last hour, between four and five. Claire was asked out by two admirers, one a new one, a man by the name of Grant, an American publisher over on an autumn visit. She had marked him down in the spring as pushy and arrogant (but clever and funny). "I'll try again," he said, "and again." He was not her type at all. She didn't even have a type now she had Robert. If she had Robert. She looked at the clock. A quarter to five.

Tom met Sarah out of school. Since he had nothing else to do this was no great sacrifice of his time and effort but he managed to make it appear so. Seeing him waiting outside the school gate – he made his waiting very obvious – Sarah thought how men were leeches. They clung, they stuck, they drew out so much energy. She did not know how the idea could ever have sprung up, already dressed to become a cliché, that men were the stronger sex. She had seen no evidence of this in eighteen years' observation. Men were only physically stronger, good at lifting dead weights. There was no man she could think of whom she admired for his strength of mind or purpose.

There were still five minutes of the lesson to go. She was in a classroom of the new block with a clear view of the gates and the park opposite and the fine skyline of London buildings beyond. The teacher was giving a final few notes on character development in *Vanity Fair*, on the weakness of the men. "You have to consider," the teacher said, "whether it was Thackeray's express intention to denigrate men. Look at George Osborne, look at Joseph Sedley, even look at Dobbin and then think of Becky Sharp. Did Thackeray call his story 'A Novel Without a Hero' because he thought no man was a hero? Anyway, before next week, I want you to have thought long and hard about the role of the man in *Vanity Fair*."

Sarah took her time getting her things together. She seemed to be thinking long and hard all the time about the role of man. Her mother, Anna, was no Becky Sharp. Anna could do with employing a few feminine wiles of the old-fashioned variety, in Sarah's opinion. A few tears. A bit of screaming. The odd faint. It might work wonders. Instead this carrying on as normal, this refusal to let Robert talk – it was getting her nowhere. Yet Sarah had found that, to her mortification, she could not bring herself to speak to Anna herself. There was an embarrassment between them which she deplored. Where and when it had sprung up she did not know. It had come, as insidious as mist, creeping up on them, enveloping true feelings, obscuring true concern. She was now part of the elaborate quadrille Anna and Robert had made of their marriage, she knew the steps by heart, could execute the formidable routines without thought. But she wanted to break rank, to force a halt. Something stopped her, something other than Anna and Robert's wishes forced her to go on with this meaningless dance.

"Hi," Tom said.

"Hello, Tom. I was going to come round."

"You didn't say you were going away. I had to come and find the fucking house shut up, hadn't I? And that cunt, Lucy what's-her-name, couldn't wait to jump out and tell me, didn't you know they've all gone to the country? Very friendly, Sarah. Nice."

"Oh, don't be so petty. I didn't know I was going. It was a sudden decision. I don't see it matters anyway."

"I have *feelings*, Sarah."

Sarah stopped dead. "Tom, if you're going to whine then for Christ's sake bugger off. I'm pig-sick of men whining."

"I only said —"

"Well, don't only say."

They went to McDonald's, which Sarah regarded with satisfactory loathing. She felt like McDonald's, all garish and chrome. The thick hamburgers, surely the most disgusting food invented, filled her with elation. With each bite she relished her own contempt for what filled her mouth. Yes, McDonald's, that was life. Her eyes sparkled with triumph.

"You're looking happier," Tom said.

"Who wouldn't be, in McDonald's?" Sarah said. "What more could a girl want?"

"Ha ha."

"You should work here, Tom. Just the sort of job you're looking for."

"I'm not looking for any job. I'm quite happy as I am."

"Liar."

"If it wasn't for the money situation, that is."

"You do like money. Such a flaw in your wonderful approach to life."

"I don't *like* it, I just need it. To eat, y'know."

"You eat. I've never seen you hungry, so don't try that. Your mum sees you eat, and drink, and smoke. You lead the life of Riley, as my dear dad would say. Eating is not the problem. It's boredom."

"I'm not bored."

"You came down to meet me out of school because you're bored to death sitting round the house all day."

"No, I didn't. I came because I wanted to see you as soon as possible. I love you, Sarah."

Sarah gave a howl, enough to make the boy at the next table drop the plastic bottle of ketchup in his milkshake. Tom got up and walked out, French fries deserted. Sarah followed him, but not without collecting his food for him. She ran along beside him as he stalked down the High Road.

"All right, I'm sorry – but I told you never to say that, you don't know what it does to me. Everyone seems to tell everyone else they love them all the time, you know I can't stand it."

"Then stuff it."

"Here's your chips. Don't be proud."

He took them, bunched them up, threw them in the gutter. Sarah laughed, put her arm through his.

"Oh, it was a dreadful weekend, Tom," she said, "you've no idea. I nearly went bananas. So wholesome, so clean, you've no idea. Just the *strain* of it. I can't sleep for worrying about them."

"Who?"

"Anna and Robert, Mum and Dad. He's so weak, Tom,

you've no idea. He doesn't know how to make a simple decision. I've watched him all weekend and it was painful. I haven't let him see it, but I've actually started to feel more sorry for him than her. He knows now, you see. She's still caught up in the dream version, he knows the reality. I mean, what *is* he going to do?"

Lily watched Anna critically. She had put the chairs up on the table, swept the floor and was now sloshing a squeezy mop over it while Anna fussed around looking for her car keys. Nerves. That was what Lily diagnosed, a clear case of nerves. Anna was all of a tremble.

"I won't be back until six-ish," Anna said, "so let yourself out when you've finished, Lily. Make sure the door is closed properly, it's been sticking. And if you could put the oven on just as you go so the casserole is ready when we all come in?"

"Right-oh."

"Help yourself for lunch. There's soup, bread."

"I don't need no lunch, I'm always telling you."

"Yes, I know, but it's a long day, you might get peckish."

"I have to watch my figure," said Lily with a raucous laugh. She knew Anna knew she would have tea every ten minutes with two sugars. "Where you off to, if you don't mind me asking? What'll I say if anybody rings, eh?"

"Just say I'm shopping."

"But you're not, are you?" said Lily, watching the suds come foaming over the bucket's edge. "If I didn't know you I'd say – I'd *guess* – you were off to meet your fancy man."

The effect on Anna was dramatic. She looked as if she were about to burst into tears. She stopped looking along shelves and into the jars that stood on the dresser and sat down suddenly on the stool beside the telephone. Her agitation ceased and she went very still. Lily was alarmed, though gratified, at the result of her words.

"Here," she said, "I was only joking. No need to look as if I'd sounded the last trump. I know you're not, don't I?" Anna could only nod. Lily began to wonder in earnest. "I should of minded my own business," she said.

"That's all right, Lily."

"What's the matter then? You're not yourself. You can't deny it."

"Lily, I think I'll have to go away for a day or so. I really think I'll have to."

"Well then, you go, why not, do you good, you're entitled."

"I don't want to."

"Don't then. Dear me. What's going on, eh?"

"You know I hate going away, anywhere. And I haven't told the children. Oh God."

"Well, Robert will cope, they'll hardly notice. Look when you went to that wedding, that friend of yours, fretted yourself to death and it was all fine, wasn't it? Eh? You're not their slave, you know. They aren't babies."

"I can't go without being sure Robert will be here."

"Of course he'll be here, where else would he be? If he isn't away he'll be here. Ring him up. Goodness me, what a Monday morning, heaven help us."

Lily was not brutal, she was merely hoping to help Mrs O snap out of it. She could not deny that all her senses were alert for some disaster and that the excitement of smelling it made washing the kitchen floor fun. Studiously she now ignored her employer, who still sat on the stool, perched just outside the kitchen door, and finished the job in hand with exemplary vigour. Anna Osgood wasn't the sort of woman who had a breakdown. She was like her, Lily thought, too sensible and tough. We could all have breakdowns if we wanted. But clearly, though not *au fait* with the finer points of psychiatric illness, Lily could see Anna was in a state of turmoil. *Could* it be another man? Lily breathed heavily, emptied her bucket, closed the kitchen door, with the window open to help the floor dry. If it was, then wonders had ceased.

"You going then?" she said to Anna, as she got the vacuum cleaner out and prepared to plug it in. Anna didn't reply. "You'll have to move," Lily said. "I can't Hoover with you in the way." Anna got up, buttoned up her coat. Lily again looked at her critically. Anna was her bread-and-butter, her point of reference, one of her few bits of luck. Life had been quite cruel enough. And Anna, faced with an accusing, bristling Lily, thought that here was someone else she could tell. Lily would listen. She would take her side – oh, to think of taking sides. But she was stopped by the feeling that only some base instinct prompted confession in this instance. Lily, unlike Gillian, would not be sympathetic, she would simply be matter-of-fact. She would advise ruthless cunning to do Robert down. Lily, no more than Gillian, would not know what she was talking about, could not possibly be of use.

She found the keys of the Mini in her pocket. Her hand closed over the sharp cold metal and prodded her into action. She finished doing her coat up. "Lily, I *am* going away, just for a couple of days. On my own. Somewhere out of London. I'm perfectly all right, no need to worry, but I'm going to tell a few lies. Necessary lies. Will you listen, just a minute?"

Betty wondered if she was a little drunk. The lunch had been such fun. It had gone exactly opposite to how she had planned but who cared? She had said her say, which ought to have devastated Robert and left her wretched, but quite the reverse had happened. They had ended up laughing. Anyone seeing them would have thought they had been enjoying a jolly joke-swapping session.

Nothing had been concluded, a state of affairs normally anathema to Betty. She liked clear-cut decisions with no room for manoeuvre. As she and Robert emerged into the cold air of Wandsworth High Street, Betty clutched at Robert's arm (though she had never before touched him, even through the thick tweed of a coat). "I won't give in my notice after all," she said. "I forgot to say. I'll stick by you. I was too self-righteous. I can't help it, it's my nature."

"I'm very touched, Betty. It's such a relief. I'd begun to feel like a murderer."

"But because I'm staying you mustn't think I approve. I don't approve, Robert. I think you could give up Claire. You'd rather give her up than Anna, wouldn't you?"

"What made you say that?"

"Well, it *is* a choice. You keep running away from it but that's because you know it *is* a choice. You aren't the sort of man who can run both. That's what this is all about, Robert: choice. Yours. Don't let anybody fool you. They're good women, Anna and Claire. They won't make the decision for you, but it has to be made, *if* you love both, *if* you do."

"Betty, why didn't you say all this half an hour ago?"

"I meant to."

She looked so stupid, standing there blinking at him, tartan beret askew, fur-collared jacket tightly zipped against the newly arrived cold wind. So stupid and yet sincere. She was speaking her mind in the time-honoured Betty way and because they had had an hour of warm companionship her words carried more weight. He supposed Sarah had said much the same thing finally but in her anger and because she was his daughter it had not registered so forcefully. Betty, he remembered, had said she loved him. She had tried to make it clear what she meant. She spoke from love. It was really very difficult to withstand this.

"Betty, I can't promise," he said, as they neared the office.

"I'd like to, but I can't. I have to see Claire first. I have to talk to her."

"It won't do any good."

"That's not the point. Things have changed. I have to try to sort it out. I'm going to her office, at five."

"You'll be late home. Shall I ring Anna?"

"Did you say that deliberately?"

"No, just automatically. You do, if you're late. Usually."

"All right then."

"I don't *want* to speak to Anna, you know, it isn't something I'm looking forward to, in the circumstances. What shall I say? She'll guess anyway."

"Oh, I'll ring, as soon as we get upstairs. I've got to try harder."

They took their coats off, hung them up. Robert dialled home. He got Lily.

Anna knew she was perfectly *compos mentis*. There was no doubt at all in her mind that she was behaving perfectly rationally if a trifle oddly. She was not a Valium case, there was not a trace of hysteria in her attitude. She packed a holdall with the minimum of things, threw it into the back of the Mini and sat herself in the driving seat. It was so fortunate she could drive. Railway stations were humiliating places to run away from – they made one feel trapped, oppressed, not free, whereas driving out on to an open road really did seem liberating.

The actual pulling away from the house was hard. Home exerted a magnetic pull upon her which took an extraordinary amount of will-power to break. She knew she would be back in two or three days but even so the going was hard. Home was her place. She was happy there. But it had come to her, as Lily came out with her coarse suggestion, that if she could not allow Robert to speak to her – if the structure of their marriage would not permit the heresies he had in mind – then she must make some gesture that was unmistakable. Robert going away amounted to nothing, it was she who must absent herself. At once, the impact would hit Robert. It would never have occurred to him that *she* might go, that he could get his breathing space or whatever he wanted in that way. He would come home and the children would be there and there would be food in the oven and clean clothes available for tomorrow, but she, Anna, would not be there. Everything would change. Robert would see her differently when she came back.

Anna tried to think of it as a holiday. The fact that she neither needed nor wanted a holiday must simply be overlooked. She was going to go to Bath, a place she and Robert had always meant to visit but never had. She had rung and made a reservation at an hotel in the *Good Food Guide* – everything was arranged. She saw herself looking round places of interest, guide-book in hand, and going to a film and enjoying a pleasant meal. Deliberately, she had chosen town rather than country. The country was too melancholy on one's own and she had set her face firmly against pathos of any sort. Brisk and businesslike, that was her intention, nothing soulful. This was to be an act of self-preservation.

Nine

Robert did not know what to think. Lily had been adamant: he must be home, please, for the children, by five o'clock. Anna had gone away. No, Lily said very happily, nothing was the matter, she had just gone away for a few days, why shouldn't she, eh? He hadn't wasted his time arguing with Lily. He doubted very much whether Anna had told Lily anything important so there was no future in pressing her but he was unable to prevent himself repeating, "You're sure she seemed all right, Lily?"

"Not when I arrived she didn't, all white and shaky like, but she seemed to get a grip. She didn't like me teasing her about going off with a fancy man – ha ha – but she got over it. 'Where are you off to?' I said to her, joking you know, 'going off with your fancy man?' and she went as white as a sheet. Course, she knew it was a joke. Have I got you worried, Mr O?"

"No," said Robert. How he loathed Lily's sense of

humour. He preferred her dark and gloomy, as she was most of the time.

"You'd have a fit if she had, eh?"

"I don't think we need discuss it, Lily."

"Don't you think she's up to it or what? She's still an attractive woman, Mr O, don't you worry. Just because she's not young no more —"

"Lily, you'd better get on. I won't keep you."

"Well, you saved me ringing you, that's one thing, one job done. She left a list, see."

"What else is on the list?"

"I've to ring Imogen's school and see she gets warned her mum won't be here when she gets in. I've to say she's had to go away sudden like, nothing serious, she'll be back soon. Course it's a lie, but I don't mind, I'm broad-minded, *and* I don't mind putting those nosy neighbours right either."

"I'll ring the school," Robert had said.

"Just as you like."

Mild tremors of alarm began to trouble him. He also felt irritated. Anna was being irresponsible. She knew quite well that of course he could be counted on to hold the fort but she was taking advantage of his good nature. Then he would have to lie, to think of lies. Lily might enjoy that sort of thing but he did not and he was bad at it. He hadn't been able to lie last week when he really needed to, for himself, and now that the lying was for someone else, and he did not understand why he was lying in the first place, it would be even more difficult. Imogen would be distressed, good God she would. She was supposed to have stability, no shocks, and what could turn her world upside-down more devastatingly than her mother leaving? She would not understand it, none of them would, they would be onto him like a pack of wolves and what was he to say? What did one say to one's children when their mother just walked out?

Of course, there was the comfort that she had said she would be back in two or three days. This thoughtless prank was not to be extended indefinitely. But it was vague. Sarah would make mincemeat of that "two or three days". Couldn't Anna have organised things better, been more specific? He would have thought she would have the decency to do so, if she really cared about him and the children. It was so unlike her not to think of the worry she was bringing upon them all, worry entirely of her making.

Then there was Claire. He could not now meet Claire and if he could not have Anna he must have Claire. He knew that thought was unworthy but he could not help it. Nor did he like to think what Claire would read into his failure to meet her as arranged. He dreaded ringing her but when he did ring and was told she was in conference and could not be interrupted by anyone he was furious. Such nonsense – in conference indeed – it was a deliberate plot to force him to turn up at five o'clock. "This is an emergency," he shouted at the girl on the telephone. "You must take a message then."

"Sorry," the girl said tartly, "no messages either, Miss Bayley said. Try again after five or in the morning."

Yet he never doubted where his first duty lay. He would be home by five. Anna had known she could rely on him, she had rightly counted on him getting his priorities right. He thought briefly of going home via Covent Garden and seeing Claire but his lunch with Betty had been late and it was already three-thirty and there was some work that simply had to be done and the drive was long enough as it was. No, there was no time. Claire could not have him in person, not today. Then his eye was caught by Betty.

By the time she pulled the door behind her – yes, it was stiff – just before four, Lily had come to the conclusion that Anna and Robert had had a tiff. The first in all the years she had known them. Neither of them had said anything but then they were both loyal, both knew the importance of keeping up appearances. Lily agreed. She had never been able to keep them up and look at the consequences. As she Hoovered and tidied and changed all the beds as instructed, as she moved about among all the Osgood things, she became more and more convinced. She had a look through Robert's suit pockets and a rummage through his desk but nothing interesting was revealed (although Lily had no clear idea of what would come under that category she felt she would recognise evidence when she saw it). But something had changed in the atmosphere of the empty house. (Common sense told Lily all that had changed was Anna's energetic absence but she was determined not to accept this simple and correct explanation.)

It was sad. Lily composed her features into an expression of mourning.

"Afternoon, Lily," Lucy said, forced to park her car yet again on the wrong side of the road. "You're looking a bit down in the mouth. What's up?"

"If only you knew," Lily said, glaring. She hated people who smiled and beamed as they announced you were looking ill or worried or down in the mouth.

"Bad as that, is it? Never mind. Is Anna in? I'm just popping in to return some sugar while I've got it in my bag."

"She isn't in."

"Oh?"

"No. She's out. Gone away."

"Really? Where?"

"That's her business."

"Oh, I didn't mean to pry, I mean, I only hope nothing is wrong, nobody ill or anything?"

"Nothing is wrong that you'd know." Lily knew she was saying more than she ought but throwing out dark hints was irresistible. The Osgoods, after all, were only mortal now, if her suspicions were right, and must pay the penalty.

"Is there anything I can do, do you think? What about Imogen coming home?"

"Her dad'll be back. Everything's taken care of."

Lucy went straight into Gillian's as soon as Lily had turned the corner of the street.

"Anna Osgood's left home," she said as soon as Gillian opened the door.

"Whatever are you talking about?"

"Anna – I just met Lily leaving – Anna's gone away, just like that. Lily seemed very worried. What *do* you think has happened?"

"Some relative taken ill, I expect."

"Wouldn't Lily have known? She said, 'Nothing is wrong that you'd know.' What do you think that means?"

"Nothing, it's just pure Lily, spreading doom. But it is odd. You would have thought she would tell one of us. What about Imogen?"

"Apparently Robert's coming home early."

"Oh well then, that's different, sounds all organised. Are you coming in, Lucy? Because I was going up for the girls."

"No, I wasn't. I just thought you'd want to know. I've been shopping, I was going to return Anna's sugar. I'll return it to Robert, later."

"Look," Gillian said, enjoying spoiling Lucy's cast-iron alibi for prying, "there's Sarah – Sarah! – Lucy's got some sugar to return to your mother, you could take it in, couldn't you?"

Caught, Lucy stalked to her car and got the sugar from the basket in the back. Before she handed it over she looked surreptitiously over her shoulder to see that Gillian had closed her door. "Here you are, Sarah. You might tell your mother I did return it – I've an awful habit of not remembering – that is, when she gets back."

"Right. I will," Sarah said.

The girl seemed abstracted. Lucy was annoyed that she did not appear to have surprised Sarah. "Did you know she had gone away?"

"Who? Mum?"

"Yes."

"I think she did mention something but I wasn't listening. I can't remember."

"It wasn't an emergency, then?"

"No, I don't think so."

"I'm glad. Anyway, I'll pop in and see if I can help out later on – tell Robert if there's anything I can do not to hesitate, I'm ready and willing, as Barkis said."

They made a performance of smiling at each other. Sarah could not get into her own house quick enough and damned the sticking door quite loud enough for Lucy to hear and feel satisfied that in spite of what had been said Sarah Osgood was for once agitated. "Mum?" Sarah called as soon as the blessed door had shut out the watcher across the road. "Mum?"

She called again as she went into the kitchen and felt hollow when there was no reply. No note, either. Everything was beautifully clean and tidy and there was a good smell of meat and herbs cooking slowly. The kettle on – the habit had to be adhered to in self-defence against a feeling of foreboding – Sarah rapidly searched elsewhere for a note. But no note. She made tea, but hung about the kitchen. Imogen came home late on Mondays, she did not get in until five, after Art Club, which she loved. Even if the world came to an end Anna would not let Imogen come home without being there herself or making sure Robert or Sarah were there. And she could not have been sure of me, Sarah thought. She never asked me, I'm never early on Mondays, none of us are. So it must be Robert.

Then she heard the key in the lock and his shout.

Claire was surprised and pleased at how well she had managed to apply herself all day. She had copy-edited almost a whole book, a job normally reserved for the peace and quiet of home; written five complicated letters to do with picture research, and dashed off blurbs for two dust-jackets. All that, and interruptions from various people wanting information of an annoyingly trivial nature. Of course, she had taken no telephone calls. She knew Robert by now. He was expert at the last-minute, impossible-to-avoid cancellation which up to now she had accepted philosophically. He was so persuasive, so convincing upon such occasions that it was merely common sense to protect herself from the possibility.

At five o'clock, then, Claire got up from her desk and began to tidy it for the end of the day. She was nothing if not methodical. Folders went into correctly marked drawers, letters into her Out tray, the manuscript she had been working on into a locked cupboard. At the back of her mind she was accepting that Robert had not turned up. His shadow did not darken her glass door, there was no sound of a heavy masculine tread in the corridor. Claire registered his absence without despair. She felt a momentary shakiness as she envisaged life without Robert, a drop in the stomach, a bleakness of vision. At no time, as she prepared to leave, did she imagine that would be that. In spite of giving her message that morning in the style of an ultimatum she was not so naïve as to assume all contact would now miraculously cease. There would be explanations, recriminations, all unavoidable. But the point was that within herself the centre had shifted. At least, she had now decided to shift it. It was no longer any good pretending that Robert could do what he liked and she did not care, no good pretending she was quite happy for him to sort himself out and do nothing herself. If Robert had achieved nothing else he had altered her own sense of perspective. Thanks to him, she saw their affair quite differently. She now wanted him, and she wanted him to herself, whatever the damage.

Slowly, she put on her jacket. She had not forgotten her promise to Anna – she would have her own justifications to work on, never mind Robert. There was a basic honesty in her that shied away from thinking about Anna Osgood too much. Always, she had kept Anna out of her mind as being nothing to do with her. She had told herself, successfully, that one could not go through life worrying about other people's happiness: one's own was quite enough of a burden. Who had ever stopped, when they fell in love, and said to themselves, "Ah, but this person is already loved, therefore I must keep away." It was absurd to consider such misplaced philanthropy. The world of love was a raw place, everyone out for themselves, everyone hungry and naked in their need. She had gone out and stalked her prey and could not feel true repentance. But what she did feel was a new understanding of what existed between Robert and Anna. She suddenly shared Anna's sense of unendurable loss. Not to *see* Robert again, not to hold him . . .

She put out the lights, looked at the clock. Certainly, there were other fish in the crowded sea. She was only twenty-two. But the sadness of rejection seeped into her soul as she stared out at the dark November sky. She became almost dreamy as she went on standing there, wallowing in her mood of melancholy. It was not entirely unpleasant. She felt like a lotus-eater, half stunned and yet blissfully sleepy, not awake to danger or pain. There was a certain relief, for the first time in her life, in not being able to do anything to direct her own destiny. She was a victim. She was simply experiencing a victim's sense of betrayal, of weakness, of bewilderment. Somehow, she had lost in a game where she had been calling the shots. Robert had not loved her enough.

And then, as Claire began to pull herself together, glorying in her ability to do so, she heard the click–clack of high heels hurrying along the corridor. Somebody's secretary, on their way home, with an urgent message to deliver. Claire stepped outside, closing her own office door. Betty almost bumped into her. "I've come instead of Robert," she blurted out. "Anna's gone, he had to go home. He didn't want you to think he deliberately didn't come. You won't, will you?"

"Anna?" Robert shouted. Sarah let him come into the kitchen and find Anna not there.

"Oh, it's you."

"How could it have been *Anna*?" Sarah said scornfully. It was a wonderful release for her own anxiety to have Robert to attack. "Presumably you knew she wasn't here or you wouldn't be home now."

"Yes, well, I thought she might be back after all."

"Where has she gone?"

"Oh, just away, for a couple of days."

"Oh yes, *just* away, I mean it's so normal, isn't it, always packing her bag and going off? For Christ's sake, Dad, have you thought about it? She must be out of her mind – she's never in her entire married life done this – no explanation, not a hint – just off. She could be ill, really ill."

"Lily says she was fine."

"Lily! Oh Gawd. Lily has about as much perception as you, she'd say exactly what Anna told her to say, she worships her, you know she does. Lily would be enjoying it – she loves drama – she's a ghoul, you know she is."

"Well, anyway, I have to believe her, there isn't anyone else who saw her go. And she must have been perfectly rational or she wouldn't have been able to organise me getting home and Imogen being warned."

"Oh, Imogen was warned, was she? That's something. Not me or Harry of course. Too much to expect."

"Don't be petty. Obviously Imogen was different. You can't be jealous of that."

"You can be jealous of anything, Dad, if you feel that way. I wasn't jealous anyway, just bitter."

"*You*, bitter? I can't see what you've got to be bitter about."

"That's your tragedy, I suppose. You never do see anything."

But Robert was prowling round the kitchen, uneasy and restless, not really knowing what to do. He looked in the oven, the bread-bin, and then put the already boiled kettle on again.

"What time do the others come in?"

"About half an hour. What are you going to say?"

"Just the truth. Anna's gone off for a couple of days. I don't think there's much else I can say – what can she expect me to say? It's her own fault."

"So you're not going to keep up a front?"

"Why should I?"

"The same reason as she did. To protect everyone, to keep this between the two of you."

"Oh, I'm not up to it. To hell with it."

"You're ready to be up all night with Imo, then? She's going to have a fit. It's her worst nightmare – Mum gone."

"That's Anna's fault. She should have thought of that."

"You think she didn't?"

"Obviously she can't have done."

"Fuck obviously. It would torture her, but you know

what she would decide? That you loved Imo therefore you couldn't be such a shit as to let her down."

"It isn't a question of letting her down – I just can't lie, never could –"

"Little whiter-than-white."

"What do you suggest I say, then? Come on, I'm tired of your smart remarks, be constructive. What do I say? She's gone on a holiday? Where? Why? In November? A funeral? Who do you want killed off? A conference? On voluntary work in hospitals? Why the hurry? Why the mystery? All those 'whys' – I'm not up to them, I can't act."

"You did pretty well, these last few months. Just carry on."

He made himself some coffee, sat with his feet up drinking it, coat still on. Sarah had almost finished her tea. She knew she could, if she wanted, save his bacon. Imogen and Harry would believe every word she said. Fluently, she could tell them of the distant relative – you know, that awful cousin we were once dragged to see – who was very ill and the wife had rung poor Mum and said she was at the end of her tether and all that stuff and of course, typical Mum, she'd said she would come, just for a couple of days, to help, to give moral support, and they live at the end of the earth – Wales – *you* must remember, Imo – that awful cottage, no telephone or hot water. It would be so easy getting the right scenario, no bother at all, every detail correct. But she wasn't going to offer it, no chance.

"What appals me," she said severely, "is what you seem to be making out of this. You just seem angry and put out. If I were you I'd be frantic. You don't seem to be thinking what it *means*."

"I don't know what it means."

"Then think about it, quickly, before the others come. Anna leaves you: what does it mean?"

"She hasn't left me, don't be so silly. Lily expressly said she would be back in a couple of days. It's only a gesture."

"Of what? To show you what? Come on, you've been married twenty years – do some interpreting."

"Sarah, I hate your attitude."

"And I hate yours."

"I regret bitterly ever telling you anything."

"Of course you do. But I don't regret you telling me. I'm glad. If you hadn't told me I would never have guessed. Does that please you? I would just have gone on thinking you were the only man in the world who really loved his wife – I would have gone on believing in a miracle and what good would that have done me? I don't feel a freak any more, that's one thing. You've always made me feel abnormal, the two of you. I've wondered ever since I was fifteen what was the matter with me that I couldn't seem to wait to meet Mr Right, that I didn't value this wonderful, unique, one-man wonder waiting somewhere in the wings –"

"Sarah, please, what you're saying is nonsense. I don't have to prove to you that it is – you know it is – you're just being deliberately cruel and sadistic. I don't know why, what you're getting out of it."

He did look very tired, deflated. Sarah tried not to relent. Then Imogen and Harry came in, more or less simultaneously, and she held her fire while she waited to see how he would deal with them. He did well, gave more or less the version she had had in her own head though he had not thought of Wales. Imogen took it quite well. Merely looked a little blank, but then rallied to Robert's suggestion that as he was home early he could practise duets on the piano with her. It sounded jolly as Sarah laid the table. Robert played well, better than Anna, and Imogen was clearly enjoying it. When Lucy came to see "if there was anything she could do" she must have been disappointed at the happy family scene.

The house fairly rang with music and laughter, it fairly shone with the candles Sarah had lit for the table in a spirit of mockery. Lucy could see no flaw, that was for sure. Robert was relaxed and easy, offered her a sherry, didn't even bother fending off enquiries, just tossed off a vague explanation and seemed not to notice Lucy pouncing upon it. Sarah called that supper was ready and as she lifted the lid off the casserole the aroma knocked Lucy flat. She had no option but to leave, voicing hypocritical contentment at the fact that they were all getting on fine. Sarah and Robert's eyes met as Harry said, "What did *she* want? Nosey thing."

Claire was so affronted she found it difficult even to be civil. "I beg your pardon?" she said, stiff and straight-backed against her closed office door.

"I'm instead of Robert," Betty said, "in case you think he didn't come." She kept pushing her spectacles back on the bridge of her nose.

"This is a little ridiculous, isn't it?"

"I suppose so, yes. He was so upset, you see, about having to dash home — for Imogen — he couldn't get a message through. So he sent me, just to say."

"He need not have bothered, how stupid. I'm sorry you were put to such unnecessary trouble. Shall we walk down?"

Claire had already set off down the corridor, furiously embarrassed. She hated Betty Munroe, ordinary, plain, loyal, impossibly virtuous Betty Munroe, knowing anything about her. It was unforgivable of Robert to involve such a plebeian person. Down the stairs they went, two abreast, Claire not being able to stand the thought of proximity to Betty in the small lift. She did not say a word until they reached the entrance hall and then she pulled on her gloves and wrapped her scarf round her neck and said, "Goodnight."

But Betty did not seem to realise this meant she was dismissed. "Could you show me the way to the tube?" she asked Claire. "I've forgotten which direction I came from, I was rushing so." There was nothing for it but to continue to walk with this unwanted emissary since she herself passed the tube entrance on her walk home. So they continued together, Betty trotting to keep pace with Claire.

"Here you are," Claire said.

"Thank you," Betty said, but still she seemed to wait.

"I must go," Claire said, to help her.

"I do know how you must feel," Betty said, in a rush. "I don't blame you, you know, don't think that. I don't know what Robert may have said but it wasn't that I didn't see your point of view. I love him too. I do *know* how you feel. It is hard, I see that. And it isn't all your fault —"

But to Betty's astonishment Claire Bayley turned abruptly away and then ran, ran, ran across the wet, dark street and out of sight.

Anna reached the hotel very tired indeed. She had never driven anything like so far in her short driving career. But the physical exhaustion was pleasant, really just what she had needed. There was no doubt about what to do with aching legs and a sore back, unlike an aching soul and sore heart. She booked in, feeling gratifyingly independent, and then ran a hot bath and stepped into it, grateful just to close her eyes and soak her weary limbs. Strangely, she was not troubled by images of either Robert or the children, not even Imogen. She seemed to exist mindlessly in a state of limbo.

When she got out and dressed herself — she intended to go down and have a proper dinner, oh yes — she was pleased to discover she did not feel in the least absurd. It seemed perfectly natural to tart herself up, to put on perfume and take care with make-up, to regard herself critically as though her appearance was of some importance. She smiled at her reflection, remembering Lily's dig about a fancy man. She supposed she could indeed be running off to meet someone just as Robert had done, except she knew he had not. Robert would never have noticed temptation unless it had been thrust under his nose. She believed utterly that he had been ensnared and succumbed: no other explanation would do. The fact that this was a convenient explanation, one that exonerated her from blame, did not escape her. She wanted to believe the best.

At dinner, she ate and drank well. There were few people in the dining room. Those that were displayed no interest in Anna, but the waiters did. She realised they assumed she had an assignation. They were accustomed to middle-aged ladies, rather over-dressed, sitting at tables and waiting. And Anna acknowledged she *was* waiting: for Robert. What had happened with Claire Bayley made no difference in the long run. Perhaps people – Lucy, Gillian, Elizabeth? – would see that as a form of self-abasement but if so they misunderstood the nature of her love for Robert, of his love for her. By an enormous effort of imagination she had succeeded in putting herself in Robert's place and that being so she was incapable of condemning him. In all her previous calculations – previous to last week – she had never thought of carrying self-identification with Robert so far.

Slowly, she finished her wine. She had done all she could do, which was not one quarter of what she had boasted all that time ago in Lucy's kitchen that she would. Her reaction had not been one of fury (as she had imagined) or of bitterness (as she supposed). She had not stormed nor laid down the law. She had had it all wrong. The explosion when it came had not found her fully protected and ready for battle. She had only seen herself fighting because she had never envisaged war. But then, on the other hand, she had not disintegrated. What she had discovered was the strength of her faith. Faith in Robert, in his truthfulness, his honesty, his honourable nature. She accepted his statement that he still loved her. What she did not accept was that he loved Claire Bayley. There, he was confused. With Robert, it had to be love to justify what he saw as his treachery. It could not just be attraction, he could not stand for that. So long as she, Anna, was at home, upholding their marriage, performing those rites of twenty years without once faltering, so long as she went on doing that, how *could* Robert be expected to admit his mistake?

The evening went well. Robert was not unused to being a family man after all, there was nothing too extraordinary in him supervising domestic routine. He was rather pleased with how smoothly the whole operation went but then Anna had left the meal ready, the children were virtually grown up, there was not after all such great cause for praise. After supper, all three of them went to do homework and he sat and read the *Standard*.

In the scramble to leave the office early he had not brought any work with him. This had been his aim for years but after half an hour he had discovered how unfortunate this was. He had nothing to do. Once the paper had been read he sat and stared at the wall in the quiet room and wished Anna would ring. He simply wanted to know that she was all right. He wanted to tell her *he* was all right, that the children were fine, that everything was going on as usual. Well, not quite as usual. Being at home was not precisely the same as usual. He did not feel relaxed or comfortable, there was no satisfaction at having reached the end of the day, no sense of reward in having got there. There was no one to talk to. Harry and Imogen would emerge quite soon but neither of them would provide the kind of talk after which he hankered. And as for

Sarah, God forbid. He dreaded Sarah coming down and finding him so vulnerable.

He could read a book or watch television. Neither appealed. He was restless, got up and walked up and down the living room. Betty would have seen Claire, told her of his difficulty, but he could not expect her to telephone. He, on the other hand, could telephone her, might be expected to. He walked towards the telephone but then halted. It really was no good. Telephone conversations were no good. He counted up the number of days since he had last been with Claire: four. It seemed much, much longer, more like a month. But then if he also counted up the number of days he had actually ever been with her they did not come to so very many. Twice a week, sometimes three times, for six months, with those three nights away thrown in. So little. Their affair hardly existed. They had not had time for anything, any pattern of behaviour, to become established. They were only at the beginning.

Three hours later all the children had gone to bed. If Robert had longed, earlier in the evening, for diversion he soon longed for it to cease once it had begun. He played snooker with Harry, watched *Not the Nine O'Clock News*, made hot chocolate all round, chivvied them all to bed at ten thirty. He went in twice to see Imogen, was relieved to find she had gone to sleep so quickly (though he knew this did not necessarily mean she would stay asleep). Then there seemed nothing for him to do but go to bed himself, among Anna's things, with the faint smell of her perfume on the pillows. Naturally, he did not sleep. The bed was huge and cold. He tossed and turned, closed and opened his eyes, sighed and groaned alternately. It all seemed so unnecessary, this disruption of normal routine, so wilful of Anna, who could not possibly be enjoying herself either. Had she hoped he would realise he would miss her, could she have thought such a reminder necessary, could she have been so crude in her thinking? *Of course* he missed her, it was so stupid of her to imagine otherwise. They were married. Married people did miss each other.

He must have fallen into some kind of doze because when Imogen screamed at two in the morning he got an appalling fright. Though he was out of bed in a second and stumbling along to her room before he had his eyes open he did not know what he was doing. He wrapped his arms round his screaming daughter and said, "Anna, Anna, there, there, you're all right, all right, you're safe." His own heart pounded with terror. Imogen stopped trembling and looked at him, huge-eyed but calm. "Did I scream?" He nodded. "You called me Anna." He smiled, made a face, shrugged. She lay down and he tucked her in, then sat by her bed waiting. "It wasn't a car," she said, "not the usual. I think it was you, something about you, Dad. I don't know what."

"Don't try to remember, it was nothing."

"Everything was blood," she said, "everything that was brown in this room was blood – the chair, the chest, my curtains, even –"

"Sssh, don't think about it."

She closed her eyes but opened them again immediately. Tears welled up. "I don't feel safe," she said, and like a baby put a thumb in her mouth.

"Well, you *are* safe." He wanted to take her to sleep with him, to comfort her, but he knew it would be a mistake. They had tried it. Instead of calming her it seemed to make her worse, more sure that she would never ever sleep happily again. The thing to do was to stay with her, just calmly sit there, until she went to sleep. Usually, Anna did it because he slept so soundly. He was surprised to find he could not remember when he had last taken his turn.

Imogen lay on her back, golden hair everywhere. She

never seemed to curl up like the others, there was no snuggling down. She lay like a medieval lady on the floor of a church, arms folded on top of the covers, body rigid under them. He kissed her on the forehead and was alarmed to find it clammy and cold. Her fear was so tangible, so vibrant in the night air (curiously, she insisted on having the window wide open, not tight closed) that Robert felt sick with misery. A child of his, so frightened, so lacking in comfort. He ought to be able to do something to restore her happiness.

When he went back to his own bed eventually it seemed even more repugnant. He hated it. If it had not seemed so feeble he would have given in to his distaste and gone to sleep on the sofa. As it was, he lay as formally as Imogen and thought about Anna. Wherever she was he felt sure she was awake too, tense and watchful in the night. It was such a waste. They could be awake together, near each other. He remembered his own night in an hotel last week and how he had longed to be in this bed he now found so loathsome, but then he had only longed to be in it because Anna was there. He had only longed to be in this house because Anna was in it. Such simple sums defeated him.

Again he dozed, again he woke but this time for no apparent reason. Half past four and all was well, officially. His head aching, he got up and went downstairs and found the whisky and drank some and felt much worse. Booze was no good, he could never find solace in it. Wretched, he made some tea and found it mildly a palliative. Wrapped in his dressing gown he hunched in a chair. The thought of the next day – today – was horrible. It would have to be got through and then another night. Before then, he must see Claire. With Anna away, there was nothing to prevent it.

Ten

They all seemed quite bright and normal, Gillian thought. Everyone appeared to go to school on time, Robert drove off to work spruce in his smartest suit and white shirt. She felt a little hurt that Anna had not confided in her about whatever had happened but she was not going to let Lucy see this.

"You do keep on about it, Lucy," she said as they sat in the kitchen after delivering the appropriate children to school. "You will see mystery where there is none."

"It wasn't normal. I just wish I'd seen her go."

"I saw her," Elizabeth said. She was standing, ready to dash, dressed for the office with her briefcase in hand, only caught because she was delivering completed work to Doug, whose accountant she was.

"Really? How did she look?"

"As she always does – well turned out, capable."

"Did she *smile?*"

"I think so. Yes, she did."

"Did she *say* anything, give any clues?"

"No. I said hello and she said hello. That was all. I must get on actually, thanks, Gillian."

"Hang on – did she have a suitcase? You must have noticed. And what exactly was she wearing?"

"Lucy, I didn't examine her appearance. I think she had a suit on – yes, I'm fairly certain – with an open-necked shirt."

"Blue? Was it a blue shirt and that blue and white silk suit?"

"Yes, I think so."

"Well. She was dressed up then, wherever she was going. She wouldn't wear that to go and see some old relative, I'll bet you any money. That's her best-occasion outfit, better than her green dress."

"Lucy, do stop it, you're obsessed," admonished Gillian.

"Didn't you ask her where she was going?"

"No, certainly not. I never ask people where they are going, it's impertinent."

"Oh rubbish. It's just friendly. If they're all dressed up, people like being asked where they are going, it's nice to share the excitement."

"I don't have that sort of mind, I'm afraid."

As soon as the door had closed Lucy mimicked Elizabeth's "I don't have that sort of mind."

"Well really, Lucy," Gillian said, "you do go on a bit."

"Do you remember when her Peter left, literally in his pyjamas after that row? I thought I'd die laughing, really Clive had to shut me up. We'd come back late and –"

"Yes, I do know. You're awfully cruel."

"But it was funny, Gillian, you know it was, you laughed at the time."

"Well, I shouldn't have done, I'm ashamed. More coffee? Then I must get on."

"Thanks. Do you suppose Anna will be back today?"

"Apparently not."

"Who said?"

"*You* said, Lucy. You said Robert thought a couple of days."

"Oh yes, I did. He seemed quite happy, you know, almost as if he was glad she had gone."

"Lucy – there you go again – that is *untrue*. You're only reading into the situation what you want to read into it."

"Did she seem normal on Friday, at the hospital?"

"You've asked me that."

"And what did you say?"

Gillian gave herself time to think. She got up from the kitchen table where she and Lucy were sitting so cosily and began loading the dish-washer. There had been something wrong with the lower rack for some time and pulling it out and pushing it in was a noisy business. What she had said was that Anna had seemed strange on Friday, unlike herself, worried, quiet, preoccupied. And Lucy could remember perfectly well what she had said, she just wanted her to repeat it in order to pounce on the words used. It suddenly seemed disloyal to Anna to repeat them. So she said, "Oh, I can't remember. I think I said she seemed fine."

"No, you didn't. You thought she behaved oddly."

"Well, what if I did? She didn't say anything significant anyway. We'll just wait until she comes back."

"If she does."

"Oh Lucy," and Gillian laughed, "you're getting carried away, of course she'll come back, she's already said she will. Why shouldn't she come back?"

"Women do run away."

"Not women like Anna Osgood. She's got nothing to run away from. You're not thinking."

"Nothing we *know* about. She could have a secret life."

"Secret from *you, Lucy?"*

"Don't be horrid. You're just as intrigued as I am."

"Yes, I am, but I'm going to struggle to contain myself. When Anna does come back she won't want to think we've been prying, or imagining nasty thoughts. She has her own life, Lucy, she *is* entitled to a little privacy without everyone jumping to conclusions, don't you think? Don't you think we should just leave her alone?"

Claire had reached home quite sick, partly with running, partly with distress. She so despised Betty Munroe. It upset her dreadfully to think Robert could have sent such a woman in his place – not just the sending but the obvious confiding in her. She had never known how Robert could stand having her in his office, could stand just having to look at that fat, bland, expressionless face, could stand listening to the monotonous, careful Scottish voice, so severe in its enunciation. Betty repelled Claire. She did not need Robert to sing Betty's virtues (as he had done). They were woefully self-evident and not rated highly by Claire. It showed her something she did not like about Robert that he could evidently relish the personality and character of his dreary secretary. For that *awful* woman to actually say she knew how Claire felt – oh, it was too much, too humiliating.

Once inside her own door Claire felt a little better but still unsettled. She walked up and down the living room, arms clasped in front of her protectively. Humiliation was something she was quite unused to and hoped never to experience again. She was determined never to experience it again. Nothing so vulgar had ever happened to her. The more she thought of it the worse Robert's action became. It was the first time she found herself thinking she might hate him, just for doing this to her, just for reducing her to the status of Betty herself. And as for Betty confessing she "loved"

Robert too – it was grotesque. Claire was frightened by her own rage.

The telephone ringing made her jump. For a moment she hesitated – it might, it surely was, Robert and she had not recovered enough to speak to him. But then a new surge of anger made her want to do just that and she fairly swept the receiver off its hook. "Hello," she shouted, and was quite thrown by the American voice at the other end. She could hardly take in what it was saying. "You're very pushy," she said, when she realised who it was.

"That's the way to gettagirl," he mocked.

"It is *not* the way to 'get' me," she said. She hated Grant. He was aggressive, smart, over-confident, the exact opposite of Robert, just as she had surmised. When she said, "Oh very well, just to stop you being a pest, but I'll meet you there," it was because she felt safe. She could deal with this, and while she was dealing with it her growing conviction that she must deal with Robert differently would harden. She needed to test and display her strength to remind herself that it existed. "Robert," she must say, "I was wrong. I do love you. And I think I know what that means. But I can't take on your marriage after all. It isn't how I thought it was. It mortifies me to tell you but you must choose: marriage or me."

But would she ever say it?

All morning Robert tried to reach Claire, all morning he failed. Betty was subdued, said Claire had not been pleased to see her. At noon, he went to Covent Garden and into the building where she worked.

He felt nervous, even shaky. The corridors menaced him. He walked along, looking for Claire's office, as directed by the curious receptionist, keeping to the wall, wishing his shoes did not sound so heavy. He really had no idea what he was going to say or how he should act. Someone would have to press a button and programme him. He was on the defensive and yet at the same time resented the fact that he was forced into such an attitude. What could Claire have expected him to do? Surely, since she had blocked his telephone calls, she must appreciate that she had left him with no alternative? Surely she understood about the implications of Anna leaving, about Imogen needing him?

He looked through the glass door and saw her, head down, writing busily. As he had first seen her. Long before he had registered the face, the body, he had noticed she worked hard, that work was important to her. Nobody would ever believe it but that was what he had admired. She was quick, original, imaginative in thought and mental outlook. She had excited him intellectually, and nobody would ever believe that either. He felt bitter that they would not. He saw now how Claire had used work to get through to him in a way that neither she nor anyone else could ever have done using physical attractions. The rest had followed.

He rapped on the glass. She looked up. Their eyes met, and it was the same: straight into him, like Anna. But she did not smile. She beckoned Robert in with a peremptory finger. He went over to take her in his arms but she turned abruptly and went to the window.

"Let's get it over quickly, Robert."

"I thought we could go out for lunch?"

"No, we can't. I can't. I'm not having lunch, I've got too much to do."

"This evening then, straight after work, for a quick half-hour?"

"Neither quick nor slow. Haven't you to get home for the children?"

"Yes, but half an hour won't hurt, Sarah can be there for Imogen. I can ring –"

"Robert, I'm not interested in your domestic arrangements, remember? I really don't want to know."

"But they're relevant. I know you're angry about yesterday but surely you see? Anna just vanished, I had no option, I *had* to go home, there just wasn't any question about it, I can't believe you can't see that."

"I do see it. I know you had to go home. You're a decent, honourable fellow and decent, honourable fellows always go home."

"Why do you say it like that?"

"I don't say it like anything. It's just a statement of fact."

"Then why are you angry with me?"

"I'm not. I'm just trying to preserve the last shred of my dignity." Her voice shook and hearing it shake and being furious with it for shaking made her speak more violently than she had intended. "Go away, Robert. There's absolutely no point in going on. I can't stand all this *fuss* any more. It isn't worth it."

She was making it easy, exactly as she had sworn she would not, rejecting him, sending him away, appearing to be self-sacrificing. 'Tis a far, far, better thing . . . She smiled, her back to him. It wasn't like that at all. She was no martyr, as she had told Anna. She believed in free choice, in taking things as they came, but she was a realist too. Robert could not live with himself if he had to give up his marriage. She would never be enough compensation. Whatever it was that had caused Robert to succumb, whatever the spur, she would never know and probably neither would he. But she would not now continue with this form of emotional crucifixion. Yet she could not turn round. It would really be very convenient if he would simply go.

Robert sat down. "I am *so* tired," he said. "I know you don't want to know about me being tired either, but I can't help it. Do I sound self-pitying?"

"I'm tired, too," she said, "and I expect Anna is exhausted. We're all so desperately solemn."

"There aren't many laughs around."

"Your Betty is a laugh."

"Claire, turn round, please. That's better. I won't touch you, promise. I see now, about Betty. Was she very –"

"*Very*," Claire said, and smiled. She knew there were tears in her eyes which absolutely must remain unshed. "But I mean it, Robert. I really can't go on. So the best thing is the long goodbye."

"I know it is. I suppose I was coming to say so but I didn't know if – you know – if I could."

"So."

"I'm scared to say anything else – I'll only put it badly – I could write to you –"

"Good God, Robert!"

"All right. That was crass, wasn't it? In the night – Imogen woke screaming, I sat for hours – in the night I felt as if I'd permanently damaged everyone's whole life, a real messenger of death."

"We *are* all damaged. It isn't like getting a sum right, Robert – there's no right answer in this mess. That was the trouble – you would intellectualise everything. It's the ruin of everything."

"It's been the ruin of me."

"But not me? I'm young, world before me, that sort of thing? Robert, I could go the rest of my life and never love anyone again. How do I know? Look, this is the discussion I didn't want. I've made my mind up. I'm *bored* going on about it, I don't want touching farewells."

"I don't want farewells at all."

"No, no, no. That's all, Robert. Go home, stay there, sleep well. I want *you* to be the one who turns round and walks out. Out."

*   *   *

After Harry and Imogen were in bed, Sarah came in late. Robert was sitting reading, pencil in hand.

"Hi."

He nodded.

"Any message from Mum?"

He shook his head.

"Great. You don't seem particularly worried."

"I expect she'll be back tomorrow. A couple of days, she said."

"You sound complacent."

Wearily, Robert put his manuscript to one side. "I'm not complacent. What do you want me to do, Sarah, weep and wail?"

"You don't seem to care much."

"Oh, shut up. You don't know what you're talking about. You're becoming a sanctimonious bore."

She went into the kitchen, made the inevitable tea, didn't ask Robert if he wanted any.

"Well, good-night."

"Good-night."

"That was Imogen last night – she screamed blue murder, didn't she?"

"As you say."

"Funny she hasn't gone on about Mum much. Have you noticed? I've missed her more." Robert didn't reply. "Of course, she doesn't know what's going on, whereas I do."

"Nothing is now going on. You can relax. Thanks for your attention and help."

"I didn't *ask* to be told –"

"As you daily remind me."

"So the *grande passion* is over?"

"It wasn't a *grande passion*. Anyway, I refuse to discuss it. I will not be seeing Claire Bayley ever again and that's all that matters."

Sarah stood in the doorway, between living room and hall, steaming mug in hand. The relief she experienced made her weak. There was a change already in her father. He looked severe, even angry, but all together again. She knew she had let him down, in his eyes, and the pity she had felt for him demanded to be shown at last. But all she could manage was a lame, "Well, I'm glad. Good. It wasn't exactly making you happy, was it?"

"I told you, I don't want to discuss it."

"Does Anna know?"

"How could she?"

"But you'll tell her as soon as she comes back?"

"I'll try."

"Please, actually tell her, Dad. Otherwise she won't ever properly know, it will go on niggling away. You must find some way, somehow, of telling her, even if she doesn't want you to. I won't mention it again, I swear, but promise? Yes?"

"Yes," Robert said.

Anna thought she would prefer to return when the house was empty, just to be in the kitchen, as usual, when they all returned from school and work. It was tempting to go back in the evening, when they would all be there together, but she put that temptation behind her. No drama, no scenes. She did not need to be clasped instantly to the bosom of the family.

She drew up outside her home at half past two. Lucy's door opposite opened at once. Lucy waved, shouted across, "Hello! Where've you been? Nothing wrong?"

Anna waved, smiled and shouted, "I'll see you later – must rush." But she did not rush. She opened the door in a leisurely fashion, sauntered backwards and forwards to the Mini, collecting holdall, coat, a book. She smiled all the time, partly at Lucy's curiosity. Inside, everything was normal –

tidy, organised. She went upstairs, found her bed in a mess (beds were Robert's weak point) and flung all the covers off to air it before remaking it later. She put on her old jeans and shirt and went downstairs to wait.

Harry said, "Oh, you're back. Where've you been anyway? Nobody tells me anything."

"I went to Bath," she said, "no special reason."

He grunted, lost interest, looked for food.

Imogen blushed, came to kiss her, clung a little, said accusingly, "You didn't *say* you were going anywhere."

"I didn't know. It was a sudden departure."

"Is the cousin better?"

Anna paused. Harry had gone. "Yes," she decided to say.

Sarah shouted, "Mum?" as soon as she opened the door and when Anna answered there was an audible sigh. She at least said, "Thank God, you're back. Did you – have a nice time?" she asked with a strange smile, head on one side.

"Yes, I did. Everything been all right?"

"Fine. Dad was in his element."

"Good," Anna said quietly. "Do you know if he's coming home on time tonight?"

"Oh yes," Sarah said, "he's coming home all right, definitely. You can kill the fatted calf – for yourself, I mean, not him."

After that, it was tense. The children drifted about, did various things, left her to herself while she prepared supper. This time last week, Anna thought, I was doing exactly the same, without thinking, without in any way marvelling at the wonder of it. Now all I want to do is go back to that innocent state. But the atmosphere in the house was different. There was not that comfortable, indifferent feeling. She watched and waited, unsure, a little remote. Everything turned on Robert's key in the lock. Which, when it came, dispelled her false calm. She could not move from the cooker. "Anna?" he shouted, and yes, his voice was hoarse and anxious. "She's back," called Harry, "in the kitchen." Still she did not go into the hall. Everything as usual, but no usual response. The Pavlovian reflex let her down. She felt very afraid.

"Anna," Robert said, standing in the doorway. (Oh, Anna thought, oh, I do love him, it would be no good pretending.) "What a fright you gave me. Are you all right?" She nodded, could not speak. He came over, said in a low voice, though there was no one near enough to hear, "I'm afraid to touch you."

"Well, there's no need to be afraid," she said, and held out her arms. They stood holding each other, quietly, for several minutes.

"Well," Robert said, and let out a long sigh. "I'm sorry, Anna. I don't understand what happened but I'm sorry. I can't say it hasn't made any difference, can I? I know I've hurt you terribly."

"Hurt yourself," she murmured.

"Hurt our marriage."

"Oh no, not our marriage, Robert. Our marriage saved us. I'm not stupid. It wasn't just me, it was what you've got with me that you didn't have with – anyone else. But I don't want to talk about it."

"I *do*, Anna – if we'd talked in the first place."

"All would have been lost."

"I want to explain –"

"I don't want explanations."

"But you'll think all sorts of things, everything will fester away –"

"No, it won't. Leave it alone and it will heal. As long as you're happy, Robert."

"Happy? I'm happy you're back. I'm happy it's all over. But I can't say I'm happy, Anna. Relieved is the nearest I can get. You're not happy either, it's impossible."

"But I am. I *am* happy. It's as if a test had been passed – the worst thing over and everything as all right as it can be, in the circumstances. I call that happy."

"That's what I want to talk about –"

"No. Please."

"If only you'd met Claire properly you'd understand better, you'd like her, she's, she was, our –"

"Supper!" shouted Anna, and the children came.

Sarah supposed Robert had talked to Anna. Certainly, they were both very relaxed. A lot of touching went on, the old show was back on the road. She watched them cynically but it was such a pleasure to have them to be cynical about. She thought she saw subtle changes already but then she was looking for them. Robert was not quite so much the adored one, that was for sure, and he knew it. A slight case of a dog with its normally very actively wagging tail between its legs. And Anna was quieter, a little subdued, more into herself. Sarah suddenly felt convinced her mother would shortly do something. What? Work? Hardly. But break out a little more convincingly than she had done up to now. Not tit-for-tat, nothing so distasteful, but a spot of rebellion some-where against the tyranny of marriage.

But at least the worry was over. Sarah felt quite tired as she went out to meet Tom. Such an almighty fuss. She regretted vaguely that she had not gone to see this Claire girl. If anything like that ever happened to her – *if* she ever got married – she wouldn't be brave like Anna. She would probably search the girl out and hit her. And hit whoever she was married to. Anna was bloody stupid to have put up with it. The Claire character was a bloody fool to let go, looking at it from her point of view, of course. And Robert was the biggest fool of the lot, as she had told him. The pieces had come together again but it was no thanks to him. Yet even as she went over it all she could not help feeling so very happy that everyone had made it. The shame if they hadn't. The waste, when there was so much love swilling about. You had to admire them, feel proud of them. If she tried hard enough she could definitely feel tears in her eyes.

Claire cried when Robert left. There seemed nothing else to do. Fortunately nobody saw her weeping so the reputation of cool and hard Miss Claire Bayley was not ruined. She cried again that evening when she got home, made herself quite ill in fact, imagining Anna reunited with Robert, then realised she was making a Betty of herself and stopped. What she must not do, she told herself, was go back over what had happened. No good tracking back to find out what had gone wrong. That way she would drive herself insane. And neither must she delude herself, make the affair shabby. Robert had loved her, for however short a time. She had loved him. It was everything else that was not simple. You can't just love A Man: The Man is what he is. You can't expect love to be enough: it is only the beginning, and Robert had had more than a beginning with Anna. So.

Sniffing, coughing, washing her face, Claire began the painful process of rehabilitating herself. Plenty of girls made it – kept their married men, won the awkward struggle within the uncomfortable confines of the eternal triangle. Wreckage everywhere, but they won. She had only been true to herself. No wrecker, no destroyer, but finding it impossible to extract what she wanted, impossible to get the pound of flesh without the blood. And the biggest stumbling block of all had been Robert's decency, his open confusion, his resolute conviction that he loved both of them. What she needed next time was a *normal* married man, glad to have a bit on the side, or else an unhappily married man, glad to have an excuse to throw it all over.

When she was old she might not care.

Betty glowed. Robert had come in singing, all smiles. The sun was back in the sky. Yes, he told her, Anna was back and everything was fine, everything sorted out. Betty said she was glad, it had all been an awful strain, hadn't it? Robert looked irritable for a moment, then agreed. Quietly, Betty began typing, the furious banging of last week forgotten.

Of course, nothing would ever quite be the same again, she knew that. Not for any of them. Robert was off his pedestal forever. But Betty was prepared to forgo a lifetime's habit and tell herself she could now turn a blind eye. Vigilance had come to an end. She felt her influence had not been negligible in the past week and this pleased her. She was not on the outside, soulfully looking in. She felt a member of Anna and Robert's marriage now, she felt a tiny factor in its survival. Thoughtfully she looked over her spectacles at Robert now and again. He needed support, she was sure. She would give it. Satisfied, Betty got on with the job.

"Well," said Gillian, "you *are* a dark horse. We were so worried, you just going off."

"Come in," Anna said. "Have some coffee."

"Hello, Lily," Gillian said.

"Hello, Mrs D," Lily said, grudging as ever. She had been quite disappointed to find Anna back. "Looks better, don't she? Better than when she went away," with a nod at Anna, grinding coffee-beans.

"I didn't see her leave."

"Oh no, that's right. Well, I saw her. Looked chronic, I can tell you. Holiday's perked her up anyway."

Gillian waited until Lily had slouched off, waited until the doleful Hoovering began overhead, waited until the coffee

was made and poured. "*Was* it a holiday, Anna? I thought a
cousin was ill?"

"Yes, it was a holiday, sort of."

"Rather sudden, wasn't it? Or don't you want to discuss it
– I mean, if it's private –"

"Oh, it isn't private. I just wanted to get away."

"But from what, Anna?"

"Everything. Just for a couple of days."

"But why? I mean, you always seem so happy and
contented –"

"I am, basically. I can't explain, really. I felt restless, as
though I needed space."

Gillian sipped her coffee. This would not convince Lucy at
all. Anna would have to do better.

"What did Robert think?"

"Oh, he didn't mind."

"Wasn't he worried?"

"I suppose he was. But he knew it was only for a couple of
days."

"And do you feel settled again?"

"Yes. Yes, I do. I'm cured. I don't think I'll need to do it
again."

"You never know. It isn't anything to be ashamed of.
Your standards are too high, Anna – you should give in
more."

"Give in? To what?"

"Just life."

Anna laughed, mocked Gillian, toasted "life" with coffee,
with gossip in the kitchen.

There was not the aftermath that might have been expected.
The first mood of relief did not give way to depression, the
first generosity to resentment. Robert did not feel watched,
he did not feel Anna regarded him with suspicion. His sense

of shame soon passed and though he knew it was thanks to Anna's magnanimity this did not make him uneasy. They never had the discussion he so badly wanted. He felt there were secrets between them, which he did not entirely like but which he was forced to respect. He was curious as to how Anna had felt, how she had coped. Constantly he tried to imagine the situation in reverse and could not. He felt guilty for years but the guilt did not, mercifully, destroy him. Guilty about Claire, naturally, but guilty about himself and most of all about Anna and even Sarah. Everyone had handled themselves better than he had, that was the truth, and he faced it. When he thought how nearly his precipitous action had brought him to total disaster he trembled all over again.

He found, as the weeks and months went on, that he still thought of Claire. Not in a lustful way, not in a way that hurt. Life with Claire would have been impossible, which she herself had known and never in the first place wanted. He thought instead about the significance of Claire. Was she visited upon him to demonstrate his frailty? Or to prove the strength of his marriage? To reassure him that he had what he thought he had? In any case, she would never be relegated in his thoughts and feelings to the position of a shabby partner in a sordid affair. The storm was weathered, but there *had* been a storm, a great unexpected hurricane which had torn through the peaceful pastures of his marriage, trying and testing everything in sight. Like all storms, it had been frightening yet exciting, it had left its mark everywhere, but it had passed and all the buildings, built of brick and stone to survive just such onslaughts, had stood firm. It had been a natural force, of the sort that can and does happen without anyone being able to prevent it.

And Anna? Lucy, Gillian and Elizabeth all noticed how thin she became, that winter. They remarked upon it to each other. Gillian, who thought everyone who lost weight immediately looked ill, saw it as an indication that Anna was not well. She thought it very silly of her to take on the Open University, was really not at all pleased for Anna when she was accepted, although of course aloud she pronounced herself delighted. Lucy wondered if the slimness might not be deliberate. Indeed, to a certain extent she had proof that it was because Anna now accompanied her to Keep Fit on Thursday evenings and Yoga on Tuesday mornings. Lucy was glad of the company, she enjoyed the slight feeling of Anna and she ganging up against Gillian. Elizabeth, who was by nature always thin, thought Anna had perhaps returned to what she had once been, the way women sometimes can after their child-bearing years are well over. She approved, she saw how plumpness had not suited Anna. But all three of them were united in one verdict: Anna Osgood had greatly changed.

Nobody challenged her with this opinion because nobody could put their finger on exactly how she had changed, apart from the slimness. She was still organised and brisk, she still had coffee with them, she still looked after Robert and the children and the house in exactly the same way in spite of her new interest in study. But she was more remote, less direct and obviously content. In some strange way she had grown apart from her friends. They were no longer so certain of her reactions. It made them a little nervous. They felt they had somehow lost Anna, but to whom? Not to Robert. She had always belonged to Robert, nothing had changed there. Lucy, who might have expected to relish this mystery, was saddened by it. She didn't know why but now that she felt herself feeling sorry for Anna she did not enjoy the sensation. Something had gone out of Anna, a something she had once found insufferable but now missed.

Anna knew something had gone. It was mourning made

her thin, a secret, gentle mourning for her own lost innocence. She and Robert were still happily married, they loved
each other more than ever, but distress had taken an
unexpected toll. They looked after each other solicitously
but concern and consideration were for a while not enough,
for Anna, that is. She never told Robert she had been to see
Claire: she was ashamed, after all. She never contacted Claire
again, nor was contacted by her, and yet she felt she ought to
have done, ought to have offered either thanks or sympathy
if only she could decide which. When, after many months,
she felt herself recovered and began to stop fretting, she felt
she wanted Claire to know how keenly she appreciated her
stance but by that time communication of any sort would
have seemed so false. She could not bring herself to make it.

The marriage of Anna and Robert Osgood endured and
was good. They were still a legend, except to themselves. If
she forgave, Anna never forgot. If he was proud, Robert
never boasted. They had both been horribly shaken by the
discovery that lightning can indeed strike twice, that all
marriages need luck as well as love, that they were after all
merely taking their chance with everyone else. They kept
their secret and prospered by it and were never found out.
The rites of marriage continued and were preserved and that
was all that mattered, wasn't it?